# THE JUNIOR NOVEL

## ADAPTED BY LEXI RYALS

Based on the screenplay by
**WILL GLUCK** and
**ALINE BROSH McKENNA**

Based on the Musical Stage play:
Book by **THOMAS MEEHAN,**
Music by **CHARLES STROUSE,** and
Lyrics by **MARTIN CHARNIN**

SCHOLASTIC INC.

ISBN: 978-0-545-79751-1

12 11 10 9 8 7 6 5 4 3 2 1          14 15 16 17 18 19/0
Printed in the U.S.A.          40
First printing, November 2014

# ONE

In a fifth-grade classroom in Harlem, New York, on the last day before summer vacation, a spunky little girl with curly red hair and a big smile read her class presentation.

". . . And so, even though he wanted to do a lot as president, he died of pneumonia after only thirty-two days. So we can all learn from William Henry Harrison to wear our coats and eat healthy so we have better immune systems. The end." Annie finished with a cute curtsy.

"Great job, Annie M.," the teacher, Mr. Romero, said. The class was in the middle of presenting their year-end reports on US presidents. As Annie skipped back to her desk, the rest of the class rolled their eyes — *that* Annie was a little bit of a teacher's pet.

"Okay, Annie B.," Mr. Romero said. "You're up."

Annie B. stood and walked to the front of the class. She had dark curly hair and bright brown eyes. Dressed in her gray leggings, pink hoodie, and hot-pink sneakers, Annie B. looked like the opposite of prim and proper Annie M.

But there was one other difference. This Annie was not holding her assignment.

"Where's your essay?" Mr. Romero asked.

"Up here," Annie replied, tapping her head. "It's more of a performance piece."

Mr. Romero sighed. Annie had never actually turned in a report, but she was great at spoken presentations.

"My president is Franklin Delano Roosevelt," Annie started. "He was elected in 1932, when most people were poor. So just like now, but without the Internet."

The class laughed.

Annie pointed to the back rows of the class. "Everyone except the front row, you be the poor people. You're all hungry and mad so stomp your feet."

The students in the back rows began stomping their feet.

"Now," said Annie, "everyone in the front row is rich. Laugh and beat your chests like you're better than everybody."

The front row liked the sound of that! Soon, the whole class was either stomping their feet, laughing loudly, or beating their chests.

"Mr. Romero, you be Franklin Roosevelt," Annie continued. When the teacher gave her a look, she flashed him a smile. "He was *very* smart."

She grabbed Mr. Romero's arm and pulled him over to the "poor people."

"Franklin Roosevelt passed a bunch of laws called the New Deal that got people work so they'd have money. He had them build roads . . ." Annie took Mr. Romero's hand and tapped one of the "poor" girl's shoulders with it. "Now you're rich," Annie told her. The girl began to laugh and beat her chest. "And bridges . . ." Annie said.

Mr. Romero continued to tap the "poor people" as Annie spoke, turning them into "rich people," until the whole class was "rich."

"He made it easy to buy a house and go to college, and before long the whole country was happy." Annie smiled. "Don't worry, rich people, you're still better than everyone, because you got even richer."

The class cheered just as the bell rang. Class was over. It was officially summer vacation!

Annie rushed out of the doors of her school, thrilled to have a break from assignments and tests for a little while. Her dark curls bounced as she pushed through the crowd of students until she found her two friends Isabella and Pepper.

"Gonna make it in time?" Pepper asked doubtfully. Pepper tended to be grouchy.

"I always do." Annie smiled.

"We'll cover for you," Isabella assured her. She reached out and slapped hands with Annie. "Good luck."

"Luck is for suckers." Annie winked.

Annie turned and jogged down the busy New York City sidewalk, her backpack jingling with every step. Weaving around pedestrians, construction workers, and deliverymen, she finally made it to a bike rental kiosk. A nice couple was returning their bikes, but Annie stopped them before they clicked the bikes into the locks.

"Do you have any time left on those?" she asked breathlessly.

"Ten minutes." The woman shrugged.

"I'll return it for you," Annie said, giving the woman her best sad-puppy eyes. "Promise."

The woman laughed and handed her the bike. "Okay."

"Thanks!" Annie called as she hopped on the bike and pedaled off of the sidewalk and onto the streets of Harlem. She wove in and out of traffic until she made it to the 125th Street subway station. She clicked the bike into another kiosk just before the ten minutes ran out and hurried up the stairs to catch the above-ground train. She pushed through the turnstile just as the train pulled into the station.

Annie sprinted, but she wasn't going to make it. Thinking fast, she whipped off her backpack and threw it through the doors, blocking them from closing. She slid onto the train, sat down, and smiled. She was on her way downtown.

Forty-five minutes later, Annie climbed up the stairs at the Franklin Street subway station. She paused for just a moment to check out a billboard for Stacks cellular phones. It promised, "No one's ever dropped a call with Stacks!" She rolled her eyes and continued on her way. There was no way her foster caretaker, mean old Miss Hannigan, would ever let her have a cell phone anytime soon.

Once she reached the top of the stairs, she sprinted down the sidewalk, turning onto White Street at a breakneck pace.

Annie finally skidded around a corner and stopped in front of a small Italian restaurant named Domani. A waiter standing inside had turned the sign on the door from CLOSED to OPEN, and was putting a chalkboard menu out front that boasted their Friday special of homemade cannoli. The waiter looked up and spotted Annie.

"Any reservations for Bennett?" Annie asked hopefully.

"Sorry, no," the waiter said. "But I'm guessing you're going to wait anyway?"

Annie nodded and sat down on the curb in front of Domani. For a moment, she clasped the silver locket she wore around her neck. Then she pulled a PB&J sandwich out of her bag and began to eat it slowly. She watched each and every couple that walked in and out of the restaurant, but as usual, none of them were her parents.

Annie had waited there every Friday night for as long as she could remember. Many years ago, when Annie was very small, her parents had left her outside a police station with a note written on a receipt from Domani. The receipt was for two cannoli, and the note on the back read: *Please take care of our baby.* It promised they would come back someday, and this was the only place Annie knew of that her parents had been to, so she always hoped it would be here. She passed the time drawing her name on the sidewalk in pink chalk.

Finally, the stream of hungry patrons slowed to a trickle, and then to nothing. It was closing time. The waiter walked out holding a takeout box with a cannoli inside for Annie.

"Sorry," he said, ruffling her hair.

"It's okay," Annie replied, standing up and brushing herself off. "I just come for the cannoli."

"See you next Friday?" the waiter asked. He knew Annie was fibbing.

"You know it." Annie smiled. Not even another wasted night of waiting could bring Annie down. Annie was an optimist. No matter how bad things got, she always had hope that things would get better tomorrow.

# TWO

"Nine . . . eight . . . seven . . . six . . ."

A countdown was in progress in front of the newest Stacks Mobile store in Tribeca. The sign out front announced: 500TH STACKS MOBILE STORE! FIRST 500 CUSTOMERS GET FREE STACKS PHONES! A huge crowd had gathered. And Will Stacks, the billionaire owner of Stacks Mobile, was standing in front.

Will just looked like the picture of success, with his flawless dark skin, expensive haircut, and perfectly tailored suit. He was handsome and famous, yet the people of New York didn't know much about his personal life. So naturally, they were fascinated with him.

"Three . . . two . . . one . . . light it on up!" Will announced. Balloons dropped from a net above the store door and a sign lit up in bright red neon. "Who wants a free phone?" Will called.

"I love your phones!" a woman near Will gushed to him. "I'm totally going to vote for you now."

Will Stacks wasn't just the owner of Stacks Mobile. He was also running to be the mayor of New York City.

He smiled at the lady. "This isn't a campaign event, but . . . I'd totally love that."

The woman laughed and shook his hand excitedly just as Grace, the Stacks Mobile vice president, walked over. Grace took Will's arm and guided him to his car.

"That's it. You're done," Grace told him quietly.

Nash, Will's security guard and driver, and Guy, Will's campaign manager, joined them as they walked down the sidewalk. Will held out his hands, and Guy squirted them with hand sanitizer.

Now that they were out of earshot of the crowd, Will didn't need to hide how grossed out he was by the germs from shaking other people's hands. "Hose me down. Put me out. Like I'm on fire," Will said, gesturing for more hand gel. He rubbed it between his palms and then over his face and down his neck for good measure. The easy smile was gone and he looked tired as he climbed into his waiting SUV.

"You kissed a couple babies. You're not going to catch colic," Grace said sarcastically.

"*You* shake five hundred hands," Will snapped at her, wrinkling his nose. "I said I wanted to help the people of New York, not touch them."

"You're helping them by providing a superior communication product," Grace said. "*That* you're good at. *This*" — Grace mimed kissing babies and shaking hands — "not so much."

"It's all sales, Gracey," Will countered like the skilled businessman he was. Then he turned to Guy. "What's next?"

"You're giving a speech to the ironworkers' union," Guy answered, checking his phone calendar.

"Ironworkers?" Will asked. He had no idea that ironworkers even existed anymore. It sounded like something out of a history book.

"If we get their support, the others will follow," Guy replied.

"Who, blacksmiths?" Will laughed. "How am I polling with witches?"

"They find you unlikable," Grace answered, keeping a straight face.

Grace and Guy looked at each other. Will was a great man, and more than qualified to be the mayor of New York City. But he was too standoffish. The latest polls said that the citizens saw him as a cold, uncaring business tycoon rather than a friendly person. Unless Will found a way to connect with the people of New York City — *really* connect with them — then he was never going to win the election.

Guy shook his head. As Will's campaign manager, it was his responsibility to make sure Will won. He would figure out a way to make it happen.

Somehow.

# THREE

Annie walked down her block in Harlem, tired and ready for bed. She passed her favorite bodega, where the owner, Lou, sat behind the counter. Annie tapped on the window. Lou looked up and smiled. He nodded for her to pick up a white plastic flower bucket by the door with a few wilted flowers still sitting inside.

"Give those to my lady!" Lou yelled after her as she walked up the block, swinging the bucket.

Annie stopped in front of a brownstone and sighed. Home, sweet home.

If the brownstone had been downtown on a nice street like Park Avenue, it would be worth millions. But this was Harlem, so it wasn't. The worn-down, shabby-looking building had been split into many tiny apartments, and Annie lived here with her foster sisters and their guardian, Miss Hannigan. It was past curfew, so Annie would have to be sneaky to get inside unnoticed.

She pulled the flowers out of the bucket and shoved them into her backpack. Then she flipped the bucket over and clambered up on top of it. Reaching, she caught the bottom bar of the fire-escape ladder with both hands and pulled herself up. She climbed the ladder until she reached a second-floor window that was open, letting in the cool night air. She raised the window very quietly and slipped inside.

The apartment where Annie and the foster girls lived was dark and silent; everyone was asleep. She'd made it! She snuck down the hall on tiptoes to her room. But just as she touched the knob, the light flashed on.

*"Come on, let's sweat, baby. Let the music take control. Let the rhythm move you. Sweat, sweat . . . freeze!"* Miss Hannigan, Annie's foster mother, sang out from the living room.

Annie took a deep breath and turned the knob. She might make it in if she hurried.

"I said freeze, you little rat! I know you heard me," Miss Hannigan yelled, stomping into the hallway.

"I thought it was part of the song," Annie said sweetly. But Miss Hannigan didn't buy it for a second. She yanked Annie down the hall by her backpack, past dozens of framed pictures of a younger Miss Hannigan singing and dancing. In the pictures, the young Miss Hannigan looked like she was a star. Now, beneath layers of smeared makeup, bleached-blond hair, and costume jewelry, she just looked tired.

Annie pulled the flowers from her backpack, petals drifting to the floor. "These are from Lou," Annie said.

"They look like they're from Lou," Miss Hannigan countered and then threw them into the trash.

"I'll tell him you loved them," Annie said.

"You always gotta be smart. Run your mouth," Miss Hannigan snapped. "You think the world wants a little smart-mouthed girl? No, or you wouldn't be here. And the only reason you are here is because I get one hundred fifty-seven dollars a week from the state. Which is not even *near* worth the torment you put me through."

Annie thought fast. She'd done this song and dance with Miss Hannigan before, and she was pretty sure she knew just how to play it. But it all depended on how many glasses of wine Miss Hannigan had had that evening. "Sorry I was a little late," Annie said contritely.

"A little late? It's three hours past curfew!" Miss Hannigan cried. "Out all by yourself in the city. And if something happens to you . . . I don't get my money! I should put you on a leash!"

Miss Hannigan lunged at Annie, but Annie was one step ahead of her. She grabbed a picture of Miss Hannigan from the table and gazed at it. The picture showed a younger Miss Hannigan singing on a stage with a famous pop group from the early 1990s called C+C Music Factory.

"You're so pretty," Annie gushed, touching the glass with one finger.

It worked. Immediately distracted, Miss Hannigan pulled the picture from Annie's hand. "I used to be a bright star. I was going to sing the number one song in the country. Getting ready to go on the *Arsenio Hall Show* . . ."

"On September 16, 1991," Annie filled in.

"And here they are: C+C Music Factory . . ." Miss Hannigan continued, not even looking up.

"Featuring Colleen Hannigan!" Annie exclaimed.

Miss Hannigan began dancing wildly and singing. Annie cheered and clapped.

"But I was too good for them." Miss Hannigan suddenly stopped. "C+C was scared of their factory. Fired me before I went on. And wouldn't let me sing." Miss Hannigan flopped down on the sofa, looking sad.

"You have a pretty voice," Annie complimented her.

"I'll die with my secret," Miss Hannigan said, tears in her eyes.

Annie slowly backed down the hall as Miss Hannigan stared at the picture. Just as Annie reached her bedroom, Miss Hannigan spotted her. "Get back here, you monster. I'm not done with you!"

But Miss Hannigan wasn't fast enough to catch her. Annie zipped into her room and locked the door as Miss Hannigan pounded on the other side. "Double chores for you tomorrow! You hear me? I'm gonna make you sweat!"

Annie shook her head and sighed. The room held three bunk beds and all of her foster sisters were awake and waiting.

"You find them?" Tessie asked anxiously. She was the worrier of the group.

"Nah. But it's okay," Annie said, trying to sound cheerful.

The girls all groaned.

"*Shhh*. She'll hear us," Tessie shushed them.

"They're never going to be at that restaurant," Pepper said.

"Be quiet," Isabella snapped at her. "Yes, they are."

"You be quiet," Pepper snapped back. "Annie's never going to find her family. None of us are."

"Don't say that," another girl, Mia, said. She was the youngest of the group at only eight years old. Her eyes welled up with tears at what Pepper said.

"Pepper!" Tessie chastised.

"Don't listen to her, Mia," Annie reassured the young girl, giving her a hug. "You're going to get adopted, I promise."

"You keep saying that," Pepper argued. "But I'm almost thirteen. No one wants a teenager."

"Yes, they do!" Annie said brightly. "We all have families somewhere."

"Can you read your note again?" Mia asked, still sniffling.

"Oh God." Pepper rolled her eyes. "For the millionth time."

Isabella hurled a pillow at Pepper. Pepper ducked and then stared up at the bottom of the bunk above her. It was covered in the names of previous foster kids who had lived with Miss Hannigan at some point. Most of the names were crossed through except the girls' in the room, whose names were at the bottom. And Pepper's name, which was midway up the list. Pepper had lived with Miss Hannigan for a very long time. She put her pillow over her head and rolled away from the other girls.

"Yeah, read it, Annie," Tessie urged. "But quietly."

The girls all got comfortable, rolling on their sides or backs so they could see Annie. Annie walked over to her cubby and pulled out a plastic bag. Inside was the old receipt from Domani with a note scrawled on the back. Annie didn't even bother looking at it. She knew the words in the note by heart:

"Please take care of our baby. Her name's Annie. We'll be back to get her soon. There's half a locket around her neck and we have the other half, so when we come for her you'll know she's our girl."

The girls all sighed. It sounded too good to be true, but they loved hearing it.

"Can I see it?" Mia whispered. She was rubbing her eyes tiredly. She held out her hand and Annie passed the note to her.

"They're going to come back for all of us," Annie said confidently. "And I bet they're wonderful."

She looked down and saw Mia had fallen asleep. So Annie tucked Mia in and put the note away. Then she climbed into her own bed and held on to her locket until she fell asleep, too.

# FOUR

A loud pounding and Miss Hannigan yelling, "Wake up, rats! Wake up!" jolted Annie from the nicest dream. She'd been eating cannoli with her parents. In the dream she couldn't see what they looked like, but she could tell it was them. And they loved her very much.

Annie closed her eyes and pulled the pillow over her head, hoping Miss Hannigan would go away.

But the doorknob turned and Miss Hannigan burst in, holding up a key and yelling, "Out of bed!"

"It's six thirty in the morning," Pepper complained groggily.

"And it's Saturday," Isabella added.

"Thanks for the time and date. Now over to Stormy with the weather," Miss Hannigan replied sarcastically. Then she held out a water bottle and sprayed the girls with cold water. "It's raining!"

The girls cried out and scurried out of bed.

"The city's coming to inspect. You gotta clean the whole place up," Miss Hannigan announced.

"Aren't they supposed to give notice?" Annie asked.

"Aren't I supposed to be married to George Clooney?" Miss Hannigan mocked.

"Who's George Clooney?" Mia asked.

"Exactly, girlfriend," Miss Hannigan said. Then she yelled, "Start cleaning! If they dock me for unsanitary conditions again, I'll ground you all for a month." Miss Hannigan turned and headed back to her bedroom. "No breakfast until this place is spotless." She slammed the door shut behind her.

"I hate her so much." Pepper scowled.

"I was having the best dream. I was ice-skating. On real-live ice." Tessie sighed.

Isabella laughed. "Save your dreams for good stuff. Like shopping. With an unlimited credit card."

"Or swimming in candy," Mia added. "Gummy bears, jelly beans, those little dot things on paper . . ."

"Or flying to the moon in a rocket — all things that'll *never* happen," Pepper said.

Just then the door swung open again and Miss Hannigan dropped a pile of mops, buckets, and cleaning supplies onto the girls' bedroom floor. "Clean like your life depends on it. 'Cause it does. And if you find any loose change, it's mine."

"Come on," Annie said to her friends once Miss Hannigan had left. "Let's get this done fast so we can go out and enjoy this beautiful day." She turned on the radio and the girls sang along and danced as they cleaned their way through the apartment, making beds, scrubbing floors, and mopping.

When they reached the living room, they found Miss Hannigan lying on the sofa watching a soap opera. "Less singing, more cleaning," she hissed at them. "And make my bathroom shine. But don't touch my medicine cabinet!"

Annie and Isabella stifled giggles. All of the girls knew that Miss Hannigan kept her stash of liquor in her medicine cabinet.

A few hours later, the apartment was spotless. The girls were all showered and dressed and waiting for the inspector. Miss Hannigan stood in front of them passing out props and orders. "You, read a book. You, braid her hair. Practice for a recital. You, put this puzzle together. It's a kitty cat."

"What should I do?" Annie asked.

"Pray," Miss Hannigan replied.

"I've tried. It doesn't work," Tessie whispered to Annie.

There was a knock at the door.

"Showtime," Miss Hannigan said. "Act well-cared-for."

"We love you, Miss Hannigan!" the girls chorused sweetly.

"*Ugh.*" Miss Hannigan rolled her eyes. "Take it down a thousand. No one's gonna believe that." She walked over to the door and opened it. The inspector waiting on the other side was young and handsome and not at all what she had been expecting. "*Whoa.* Well, hello there."

"Excuse me?" the inspector asked.

"Nothing," Miss Hannigan said brightly. "It's just, most inspectors are old and not rock-star gorgeous."

The inspector wasn't fazed. "Are you Colleen Hannigan?" he asked matter-of-factly, looking down at his clipboard.

"My maiden name. But I'm not married to it. If you know what I mean," Miss Hannigan replied flirtatiously. "Come on in. The girls are just recreating."

The inspector walked in to find the girls playing and acting happy. "How's everyone doing?" he asked.

"Just living the dream." Annie smiled sweetly.

Miss Hannigan took the inspector's arm and led him toward the kitchen. "Can I offer you something to drink? Skim milk? Kale smoothie? Fresh-squeezed orange juice?"

"I'm fine, thanks. Let's start in the bathroom?" he suggested.

As they headed down the hallway, the inspector dropped a piece of paper from his clipboard.

Pepper bent down and picked it up. She read it quickly. "This has all our information on it."

All of the girls rushed over to look at it.

"I've been in a lot of homes," Isabella said, pointing at her name.

"This says I've been in millions," Tessie exclaimed.

"That's your Social Security number, dummy," Pepper told her.

"What's a scocial scasurty murder?" Mia asked.

Isabella laughed. "It's what you need to apply for a credit card."

"Wait!" Annie exclaimed. "I can use this to get my records. And find my parents."

"I'll copy it down," Tessie said, scrambling to find a pen and paper. "Plan your exit."

Annie, with her information carefully folded up in her pocket, headed down the hall to make her escape. She paused outside the bathroom and listened. Miss Hannigan was still trying to flirt with the good-looking inspector, who didn't seem interested in the slightest.

Annie stuck her head into the bathroom. "Can I go to the library to study?"

"Let's talk about it after the handsome inspector with no wedding ring is gone, okay?" Miss Hannigan answered through clenched teeth. "Now, run along."

"Okay," Annie said, thinking fast. "But first, can I have some floss? I got some nutritious breakfast stuck in my teeth. Pretty sure I saw some in the medicine cabinet."

The inspector pointed to the medicine cabinet. "In here?" he asked.

Miss Hannigan, looking panicked, scurried in front of the inspector before he could open the cabinet. She shot Annie a nasty look. "I think we're out. Why don't you pick some up on the way to the library?"

"Thank you, Miss Hannigan!" Annie beamed. Then she turned and skipped out of the bathroom.

Miss Hannigan glared at her and then turned to smile at the inspector. "I don't do this for them, they do this for me. I'm really a singer — I'm just between gigs at the moment. The kids keep my feet on the ground."

Annie raced down the street to Lou's bodega, grinning broadly. Lou was sitting behind the counter and looked up when he saw her come in. The walls of the shop were covered in old head shots of Miss Hannigan from her performance days. There was also one picture of Miss Hannigan and Lou together, signed: *Lou, Thanks for always looking out, Colleen.*

"Uh-oh. I know that run. How much you need, *mija*?" Lou asked. That was Spanish for "my girl."

"Forty-three fifty-five," Annie said hopefully.

"By when?" Lou asked.

"Now?" Annie replied, still looking hopeful.

Lou laughed. "Go rob a bank. I can loan you my mask."

"Please, Lou. I think I'm close to finding my parents." Annie gave him her best puppy-dog eyes.

Lou sighed. There was no way he could say no to Annie. "Take out the expired drinks from the cooler."

"Thank you, thank you, thank you!" Annie exclaimed. She grabbed the trash can and started to drag it over to the cooler.

"What are you doing, girl? Don't throw them out. Change the date," Lou instructed and then tossed her a pen.

Annie smiled and sat down on the floor, stacking drinks and watching TV with Lou.

Meanwhile, in Brooklyn, Will Stacks was giving a speech at a soup kitchen in front of a gaggle of reporters.

". . . I believe in hard work. Never settling for okay. Great is all I know. That's how I built my company into a worldwide leader. And that's what I'm going to do with this city. Make it great again."

"You're twenty points down in the polls — your billions don't seem to be working. How do you plan to change people's minds?" a reporter asked.

"At Stacks Mobile I made a cellular network that never drops a call. As mayor, I'm going to make a government that never drops a citizen," Will answered smoothly. "But enough politics. Let's let these good people eat, huh?" Will straightened his tie and walked over to Grace and Guy. "I hate this," he said in a quiet voice. "For the record, I really hate this."

"Let me just check the record," Grace replied with light sarcasm. "Oh, look, there I am, last year, saying: 'You shouldn't do this. You will hate this. You will really hate this.'"

Will sighed. "It'll all be worth it when I win."

Grace shook her head. "So is *this* the thing that will make you happy and complete?" she asked. She knew Will was a good man and that he needed something more in his life. But in her opinion, running for mayor wasn't it.

Guy looked up from reviewing the video of the

speech on his tablet. "You only smiled four times. You've got to bump that up. Voters respond twenty-three percent more favorably to full-teeth smiles."

"How do they feel about thumbs-ups?" Will asked.

"Sixteen percent better if you give a single, thirty-eight percent if you shoot them the double," Guy replied. Then he shot Will a double thumbs-up to demonstrate.

"Am I going to win, Guy?" Will asked more seriously. "'Cause I don't like wasting time."

"You hired me to win. You'll win," Guy answered just as seriously. Then he handed Will an apron and a hairnet.

"Whoa, what are you doing?" Will asked.

"You have to serve them," Guy replied.

"The hoboes? Are you serious? Why?" Will wrinkled his nose as he put on the hairnet. It was really a shame to cover up such a gorgeous head of perfectly cut hair.

Grace smiled at him. "Because for some crazy reason, everyone thinks you're a rich elitist who can't connect with regular people."

"*You're* telling me to 'keep it real,' Miss 'I Went to Oxford,'" he grumbled at her.

"I'm just telling you that if you want any chance,

you have to remember where you came from. Okay?" She helped him tie the apron on.

"Make sure you compliment the food, but not too much," Guy instructed.

"I'm not eating that food," Will stated.

"You're *going* to eat the food," Guy replied firmly. "Say it's good, don't say great. And take seconds, but only eat half, or it'll seem like pandering."

"How do you sleep at night?" Grace asked Guy.

Guy just smiled. This was nothing. To him, running a campaign was second nature.

Twenty minutes later, Will stood at the buffet line, serving out bowls of soup to Brooklyn's homeless. He was smiling and laughing with the other volunteers and making small talk with each person he served, but there was something about him that just seemed awkward. The reporters were snapping pictures and taking notes.

"Bet you never had mashed potatoes," one of the homeless men said to Will.

"Are you kidding?" Will asked. "My grandma made the best mashed potatoes. Best in the Bronx." He looked over the man's shoulder and caught Grace's eye. "Did you know I was from the Bronx? Born and raised. These look pretty good, though — not amazing, but not terrible."

Will took a big bite of the mashed potatoes, and then immediately spit them back out all over the people waiting in line! They looked at him in shock while Will coughed and patted his chest with his fist. "Went down the wrong pipe," he said, gagging a little. But the photographers had already taken picture after picture.

Will took a sip of water and then gave it a second try with another bite. He did his best to swallow, but he just couldn't do it. He spit all the potatoes out again. "These are disgusting!" he exclaimed as more cameras flashed.

So much for seeming relatable.

Once inside the car, Will looked at his team sheepishly. "So how do you guys think that went?" he asked. "Nash, you saw it. Would you vote for me if you didn't work for me?"

"No, sir," Nash answered without missing a beat.

"Thanks for your honesty. You're fired," Will replied, joking.

Nash smiled.

Grace looked up from her tablet. "That didn't take long." She held it up. A video of Will spitting on the homeless man was playing on the screen. It had gone viral. "And there are already parodies," she added, swiping through to show videos of Will spitting on kittens, pandas, and even the president.

She shrugged. "This might be a blessing in disguise. Just because you *can* run for mayor doesn't mean you should."

Will shook his head. "We've been through this — the bigger my profile, the better for the company. And also, the city needs my help."

"Okay, Batman," Grace joked.

"You let all your employees talk to you like that?" Guy asked, raising one eyebrow.

"Just the ones who've made me billions of dollars," Will replied.

Suddenly, the car jerked to a stop. Nash tried to restart it, but it was no use — something was wrong.

# SIX

Annie waited as patiently as she could in line at the Family Services Office. She couldn't believe she was finally going to get to see her records. It was just the breakthrough she had been hoping for.

After what seemed like forever, she reached the front of the line and was called forward by a government worker whose name tag said: MS. KOVACEVIC.

"I'd like to get my records, please," Annie said politely.

Ms. Kovacevic didn't look up. "You need DOH form number four-three-eight-zero —"

"Point-seven-dash-A," Annie finished for her and handed over the completed form.

Ms. Kovacevic raised an eyebrow. "And forty-three dollars and —"

"Fifty-five cents," Annie cut in and handed over the exact amount in cash.

"Application signed by a parent or —"

"Guardian." Annie reached over and pointed at the line on the form signed by "Colleen Hannigan" in somewhat childlike writing.

Ms. Kovacevic nodded. She turned and began typing Annie's info into her computer while Annie watched her every move.

"Are you going to stare at me the whole time?" Ms. Kovacevic asked, clearly annoyed.

"Sorry," Annie said and then waited patiently until Ms. Kovacevic turned back and handed Annie a sheet of printed paper — her records! "Can you read it? I'm too nervous," Annie asked.

Ms. Kovacevic sighed. "Annie Bennett, abandoned outside the Twenty-Sixth Precinct. Age estimate: four years. Placed in state foster care. No further data."

"What does 'no further data' mean?" Annie pushed.

"It means that's all there is to know about you. Sorry, honey." Ms. Kovacevic gave her a tight-lipped smile and then turned back to her computer.

"It's okay, I'll figure it out," Annie said and forced a smile of her own.

But outside, she couldn't help tears welling up at the corners of her eyes. She started heading home through a small park. She was really disappointed. This was supposed to be the day that she'd get a good lead on her parents.

After a moment, she brushed away the tears. There was no use in feeling sorry for herself. Today may not have been the day, but there was always hope for tomorrow!

As she walked out of the park, a cute little dog ran past her. The dog kept stopping to spin in place, chasing her tail. Annie laughed just watching her. But two teenage boys threw some bottles at the poor pup, chasing and taunting her.

"Hey!" Annie yelled and took off running after the boys. She wasn't going to let them hurt a cute little puppy.

Will's SUV was toast. The engine wouldn't start and there was nothing Nash or Guy could do to fix it.

"I'll call for another car," Grace announced as Nash closed the hood.

"I think I'm going to walk," Will said.

*"What?"* Guy and Grace asked at the same time. They were stunned. Will had always preferred a private car.

"I want the air." Will shrugged.

"I'll go with you," Guy told him.

"No," Will said, waving him off. "I want to be alone."

Grace whipped out her phone. "I'll text you directions."

Will shook his head and started walking. "I know how to walk down a street," he called over his shoulder.

"Leave her alone!" Annie cried as she chased the boys chasing the dog. But they paid no attention to her.

She ran across a side street without even looking for traffic. She was having a hard time keeping up. She almost lost them a couple of times but finally spotted them again — they had the dog cornered down the next alley. The pup spun again, chasing its tail.

"I told you to stop!" Annie yelled.

Will hadn't been on a walk in a long time — at least not a walk out on public sidewalks — and he had just remembered why. He couldn't go anywhere without being recognized.

A garbageman hanging off of the back of a truck had shouted, "Your phone bill's killing me, bro!" as he drove by. And some pushy woman had run up to snap a selfie with him before he could stop her. "I'm taking a picture of Stacks on my Stacks!" she'd squealed to her friends.

Between the whispers and the photos, Will was ready for his walk to be over. He trained his eyes on the ground and picked up the pace.

As Annie hurried to get to the alley, Will rounded the corner and the two of them ran smack into each other. Annie fell backward into the street and landed flat on her back. A van was barreling toward her! It slammed on its brakes, but it wasn't going to stop in time.

Will didn't even hesitate. He darted into the street and dragged her out of the van's way. He had saved Annie's life!

"Whoa," Annie said breathlessly as she turned to look at her rescuer.

"You okay?" Will asked.

"Yeah," Annie said. She stood up and frantically scanned the sidewalk for the dog. The boys chasing it had been distracted by her dramatic rescue and the little dog had used the opportunity to run out of sight around the corner. She was okay. Annie smiled.

"You could have gotten run over," Will chastised Annie.

"Sorry." Annie shrugged.

"Don't be sorry, just be careful," Will told her. "Why are you running anyway?"

"Gets me places quicker," Annie said with a smile. Then she turned and jogged down the street toward home.

Will shook his head. "Little kids."

He continued on his way, totally oblivious to the man behind him who had just recorded the whole incident on his Stacks cell phone.

# SEVEN

When Annie got home, she found Miss Hannigan working out in the living room using an old piece of exercise equipment.

"How was the library?" Miss Hannigan asked sarcastically.

"Educational," Annie replied.

"Well, here's some more education for you." Miss Hannigan stopped exercising and scowled. "I told Family Services I don't want to foster you anymore. As of next week, you're somebody else's problem."

"Did they say who?" Annie asked, looking hopeful.

"Not a *who*, sweetie. A *what*. Group home. I think it's in Albany. Or Schenectady. Some place ending in

*Y.* As in, 'Why are there three hundred kids sharing one room?'"

Annie shook her head, trying not to cry. She didn't want to give Miss Hannigan the satisfaction of seeing her upset, so she turned and hurried to her room.

"Maybe this will teach you to stop running your smart mouth!" Miss Hannigan yelled after her.

Far away from Harlem, Will Stacks was in his office. The room was state of the art. It was equipped with all of the latest technology and it had amazing views of downtown Manhattan — not that Will noticed. He was too busy working.

"We got the cell-phone battery to last up to one hundred fifty hours," Grace reported as she scrolled through an e-mail on her computer.

"That's not a week," Will said, frowning. "I wanted a full week without a recharge."

"I know. We'll get there," Grace assured him. "But right now it's burning people's hands."

Just then a video-message screen popped up on Will's laptop. It was Guy calling.

"What's up, Guy-O?" Will answered.

"*You're* up. Five points in the polls!"

Will had never heard Guy sound so excited.

"People liked that he vomited on a homeless man?" Grace asked, confused.

"No, you saved a little girl from getting hit by a van. Someone recorded it and it's gone viral!" Guy explained. He pushed a few buttons on his phone and a video box popped up on Will's screen showing the clip of Will saving Annie. "This is fantastic, Will. First time this campaign you've done anything vaguely human. All due respect."

"You didn't tell me you saved a little girl." Grace looked at Will. "You never tell me anything."

"Like Batman," Will said, joking.

"We have to capitalize on this," Guy announced, already making plans. "You invite her to lunch, see how she's doing, snap a few pics. The press will eat it up!"

"Do we know who she is?" Will asked.

"That's the best part. She's a foster kid. Lives in Harlem. How perfect is that? *Foster kid! Harlem!*" Guy was ecstatic.

"Your neck vein is bulging," Grace commented. She

clearly thought his campaign tactics were less than likable.

"I'm going to go get her," Guy continued as if she hadn't spoken.

"Not you. Grace," Will told him.

Grace raised an eyebrow. "Why me?"

"Would you want 5-Hour Energy showing up at your door?" Will asked, gesturing toward Guy's face on the screen.

Grace tried to protest, but Will flashed her one of his most convincing "everything will be fine!" smiles. She sighed. When it came to Will Stacks, she had a hard time saying no to his plans, even if they were crazy.

Grace knocked politely on the door to Annie's apartment.

"Yeah?" Miss Hannigan's voice yelled through the intercom.

"Is this Colleen Hannigan?" Grace asked. "I want to talk to you about a girl in your care. Annie."

*"Uggghhh,"* Miss Hannigan groaned. But she pulled

the door open. "You can take her today, but I want to get paid for the month. I already bought her food."

"I think you've mistaken me for someone else," Grace told her. "I work for Stacks Mobile."

Miss Hannigan looked around surreptitiously and lowered her voice. "It's not my fault I went over my Anytime minutes last month. I didn't know that guy was in Sri Lanka."

"This isn't about your phone bill. I'm here on behalf of Will Stacks," Grace continued. "He'd like to invite Annie to lunch."

"What? Why?" Miss Hannigan demanded.

"They ran into each other yesterday. Annie didn't tell you?"

"She never tells me anything," Miss Hannigan said, doing her best to be charming. "We didn't get a chance to have our girl-talk jawbone last night." She yelled for Annie and then turned back to Grace with a calculating glint in her eye. "He ran into her, huh? You know, her neck did seem a little whiplashy."

"We'd also like to make a donation to the charity of your choice," Grace added.

Miss Hannigan let out a long, dramatic sigh. "So many to choose from. Save the Whales . . . Clean

Water . . . You know what? Just make it out to 'Cash' and I'll divvy it up." Miss Hannigan eyed Grace's checkbook greedily. Then she turned and yelled again, "Annie! Get out here!"

Annie came out of her bedroom, pulling on a hoodie.

"You're going with this lady," Miss Hannigan said, pulling Annie to her in a tight hug and pretending to sound like she cared. "Is that okay, sweetie?"

Grace bent forward so that she was at Annie's eye level. "Hi, I'm Grace. I'd like to take you to lunch. I promise I won't keep you long."

"You can keep me as long as you want," Annie assured her, looking delighted.

Grace led Annie downstairs where Will's SUV was waiting for them. Annie's foster sisters trailed after them, in awe of Annie's good fortune.

"No way!" Tessie exclaimed when she spotted the car.

"Is this for real?" Isabella asked.

"You're so lucky!" Pepper said jealously.

Annie just smiled and climbed into the SUV. She couldn't believe her eyes. The car was fully loaded with bottled water, sodas, candy, gum, magazines, and snacks. She had never seen a car with so many treats!

"Help yourself to whatever you want," Grace told her as she took her seat.

"Really? Thanks!" Annie exclaimed. She grabbed handfuls of treats, rolled down her window, and handed them out to her friends waiting outside.

"Maybe I should come with you? Make sure everything's USDA Grade-A Awesome?" Miss Hannigan called down from an open window.

Annie laughed. There was no way she was letting Miss Hannigan ruin this. "I'm good!" she yelled as they drove off.

Lou walked over as the girls ran back into the building, eager to eat all the candy. "Hey, gorgeous," Lou yelled up to Miss Hannigan. "How does it feel to have a famous kid?"

"What?" Miss Hannigan asked him, genuinely confused.

Lou held up a copy of that day's paper with a photo of Will Stacks saving Annie on the cover.

*"Arrgh!"* Miss Hannigan screamed. If there was one thing that bugged her more than not being famous, it was seeing *other* people get famous!

# EIGHT

Annie had never been inside such a cool car. In addition to the awesome snacks and free sodas, there was a touch screen that controlled the in-car entertainment system. She swiped through the buttons, finally selecting a news program on a talk radio station.

"Are you sure you don't want to listen to music?" Grace asked, raising an eyebrow at Annie's choice.

"I love talk radio. It calms me," Annie insisted and then buckled herself in.

Once Annie was settled back in her seat, Grace turned to her. "Mr. Stacks would like to take a few pictures with you, if that's all right."

"I guess so. Why?" Annie asked.

"Well, people want to know you're okay," Grace told her.

"What people?"

"Everyone who saw that," Grace answered and then pointed to an electronic billboard outside the window for a local news station. It showed an enlarged picture of Will rescuing Annie.

"Whoa!" Annie gasped. "My hair is gigantic!"

Annie glanced out the car window and noticed that other people were staring up at the billboard, talking and pointing.

She was starting to get the feeling that today was going to be about much more than just lunch.

Annie couldn't believe her eyes when she arrived at Will's office. There was a buffet set up with more food than she had ever seen at once — all of it served on china and crystal.

"Annie!" Will greeted her warmly, reaching out to shake her hand for the small crowd of photographers waiting at the edges of the room.

Annie had prepared for this. She'd been thinking

on the car ride over. A guy this important didn't just invite someone to lunch without an angle. Annie knew something was up.

"Slow your roll," she said.

"Excuse me?" Will asked, surprised.

"Can we sit down first?" Annie asked.

Will turned and looked at his team for guidance. Grace just shrugged. Guy looked annoyed, but nodded. So Will waved the photographers away to get some lunch and led Annie over to a table. "Are you okay from yesterday?" he asked kindly.

"I'm fine, thanks," Annie replied. "So what's the hustle?"

"What?" Will asked. Either this was a very strange little girl, or a very smart one.

"You picked me up in a space car, brought me to James Bond's house to eat . . ." Annie trailed off and examined the lobster on the platter in front of her. ". . . giant bugs. I'm guessing it's got to do with that photo of us. I'm ten, I'm not an idiot."

Will was surprised — she *was* smart. "I didn't say you were an idiot," he answered. "Or ten. I have no idea how old you are."

"I'm ten," she assured him.

"Okay, so you're not an idiot," Will agreed. "But a lot of people are, and when they saw that photo they thought I'd be a good mayor."

"Why?" Annie pressed him.

"I'm a rich guy, you're an orphan . . ." Will started to explain.

"I'm not an orphan. Foster kid," Annie corrected him.

"Let's just say that the more that people see us together, the better it is for my campaign," Will finished.

"*That's* how a mayor gets elected?" Annie was shocked.

"I know, it's insane," Will agreed. He took a sip of water.

"I bet if I moved in with you, you'd become president!" Annie exclaimed.

Will laughed and spit his water across the table, choking.

"I saw *that* photo, too," Annie told him, referring to Will spitting on the homeless man at the soup kitchen. "Why do you do that? Is it like a throat thing?"

Just then Guy came rushing over. He'd been listening in on their conversation.

"That's not a bad idea," Guy said. "Annie staying with you." He paused for a moment at the incredulous looks on Will's and Annie's faces. Then he turned to Annie. "From what I understand, it's pretty crowded where you live now. How about a little more space? Is that something you might like?"

"Living with a billionaire?" Annie replied. "I'll allow it."

"See? It's perfect." Guy nodded enthusiastically.

"What are you doing?" Will hissed at Guy.

Guy took Will aside. "It'll just be for a few weeks, then she'll go back," he whispered. "Take in a foster kid? Fifteen-point jump in the polls, guaranteed!"

"So you want me to play daddy?" Will asked louder.

"It's easy. All I need is a bed and meals," Annie assured him. "You don't have to do anything else. And you get one hundred fifty-seven dollars a week."

Will looked over to Grace for guidance but she just shrugged.

"You want photos, right?" Annie continued. "This is a way to get *a lot* of photos." She jumped up, put her arm around Will's shoulders, and posed for the photographers, hamming it up for the cameras.

"There are easier ways of getting photos," Will said.

"Not with me in them," she countered and then went back to posing happily.

Grace pulled Will and Guy to the side while Annie loaded up her plate to eat. "Are you really doing this?"

Will nodded. "I won't even know she's there. It's like having a turtle."

"I wonder if she has her shots," Guy mused.

Annie, meanwhile, was practically jumping for joy on the inside. Living with a billionaire was *way* better than going to some crowded group home in Albany. And even if it wouldn't last forever, it would give her time to come up with a new plan. Maybe even find her real parents.

Today was turning out to be a pretty great day.

# NINE

Before she knew it, Annie was back at the New York Family Services Office. But this time she had Will, Grace, and Guy with her.

"I can't remember the last time I stood in line," Will said, looking around at the drab office.

Annie shook her head and smiled. "That's the kind of stuff you need to stop saying if you want to get elected."

Just then a man walked over and took a picture of them with his camera phone. Will flashed him a double thumbs-up and Annie gave a dazzling smile. A few pictures later and they found themselves at the front of the line.

"I need a temporary guardian approval," Annie announced when she walked up to the desk, only to find herself face-to-face with Ms. Kovacevic again.

"There's a six-week waiting period and you need form NYS eighty-four dash —" Ms. Kovacevic stopped mid-speech when she looked up and saw Will Stacks. "Sweet Lord."

"Recognize," Annie said.

Thirty minutes later, Ms. Kovacevic escorted Annie, Will, Guy, and Grace to Will's apartment to do an inspection.

"I normally don't do site visits," Ms. Kovacevic told Will. "But I've taken a liking to young Annie. I forget sometimes why I got into this." Then she pulled her phone out and took a selfie with Will in it. "For the files," she assured him as they walked into the elevator.

The elevator had a touch screen that recognized the handprints of Will and his most trusted assistants. Will scanned his handprint and pressed the electronic button for PENTHOUSE.

Ms. Kovacevic looked down at her clipboard and read from the form, "Does the guardian have adequate income to provide basic shelter? I'm going to go ahead and check that box as 'yes.'"

The elevator dinged and Will held the doors open as everyone walked out into his penthouse apartment. "Come on in."

As soon as Will spoke, the apartment came to life. The window blinds rose, revealing amazing views of Manhattan. The lights came up and the air-conditioning kicked on.

"Whoa," Annie exclaimed in awe.

"It's a smart house," Grace explained. "It recognizes Will and changes accordingly." She turned to Annie and held out her phone. "Let's get it to learn your voice. Speak into this."

"What should I say?" Annie asked.

"Anything!" Grace replied.

"I think I'm going to like it here," Annie said into the microphone.

"Got it." Grace smiled, looking down.

"Is there a co-temporary guardian?" Ms. Kovacevic asked Will.

"No," Will replied over his shoulder.

"Would you like a co-temporary guardian?" Ms. Kovacevic flirted.

Just then Will's cell phone rang and he was saved from answering Ms. Kovacevic.

"Take it," Grace told him, waving him off toward the office. "Someone has to do some real work for the company today."

"I'll come with you," Guy said, following Will out the door. "Want to talk about a new campaign. Featuring Annie."

With Will gone, Ms. Kovacevic looked back at her clipboard for all the items she needed to see in the apartment. "I need to see the kitchen, ventilation, at least one sink per four persons . . ."

"Come with me," Grace cut her off. She took Annie and Ms. Kovacevic through the entire apartment, pointing out all of the cool features. There was a hot cocoa machine that made the perfect whipped-cream topping, and any wall could become a TV screen with a tap on one of the wall tablets. There was a tennis court on the roof and even an indoor swimming pool!

But the best part of it all was that Annie had her very own room. It had a king-sized bed and a view of the Empire State Building. Annie had never had a room all to herself. As she jumped backward onto the down-filled mattress, she realized she *was* going to like it here — a lot!

# TEN

That afternoon, Annie went back to Miss Hannigan's apartment to pick up her things. "The closet was so big, I thought it was the living room," she told her foster sisters as she stuffed clothes into her backpack.

"How big was the living room?" Isabella asked.

"I thought it was the street!" Annie exclaimed.

"Is he nice?" Tessie asked wistfully.

Annie paused. "I think so. He just doesn't know it."

"I'm going to miss you." Mia sniffed.

"I'm not," Pepper said. "Finally, we'll get a little space in here."

"Well, whenever you miss me, all you've got to do is call." Annie pulled out four brand-new Stacks phones — one for each of the girls. "Bam. Even for you, Pepper. I know you're going to miss me."

"Oh my gosh!" Tessie squealed.

"Thanks, Annie!" Isabella and Mia chorused.

"No case?" Pepper asked. But deep down, she was thrilled with the present. And she really was going to miss Annie.

Downstairs, Will waited for Annie in his SUV. He was working diligently on his tablet when a rapping on the window caught his attention. He looked up to see Miss Hannigan knocking. "Hey, Mr. Will Stacks," she said super-flirtatiously. "Or should I say Mr. Soon-to-Be-Mister-Mayor."

"No thanks. I'm just waiting for someone," Will called back, keeping the window firmly up.

Nash got out of the front seat and came around to shoo Miss Hannigan away. "Ma'am, you want to move on? Thanks."

"What? No!" Miss Hannigan was furious. "How dare you. I'm a music superstar!"

Just then Annie and the other girls came running out to the car.

"Hey, Miss Hannigan," Annie said seriously. "I just want to thank you for everything you've done for me —" Annie couldn't finish her sentence because she burst into giggles. "I can't do it with a straight face. Peace out."

Miss Hannigan stomped her foot and glared at Annie. "You think your life's a fairy tale? There *is* no happily ever after! The worst thing in this world is a little taste of something good. Because it never lasts, and all you taste from then on is not-that-taste."

"Huh?" Mia asked.

"*Shhh.*" Pepper patted Mia on the head. "Just let her talk when she gets like this. Remember?"

The girls hugged Annie good-bye and then she climbed into the car.

"Who was that?" Will asked.

"Exactly," Annie replied sassily, but she turned back to wave to her foster sisters as the car pulled away.

"Where's all your stuff?" Will asked, looking around for a suitcase or duffel bag.

"Right here," Annie replied, holding up her

backpack. "Wait." She checked her pockets. "Yup. Got everything."

"The usual?" Nash asked her.

"Please." She smiled.

Nash turned on the talk radio station just as the car stopped at the red light at the corner. Lou came over and knocked on the window.

Will looked up, startled. "No, thank you!" he yelled at Lou and then hissed at Nash, "Run the light."

"Wait! That's Lou," Annie exclaimed and then rolled down the window. She pulled another phone out of her pocket and tried to give it to Lou. "I got this for you."

"No thanks, *mija*. Those things are evil," he told her. "They steal your private information so big business can spy on you and crush your soul." He gestured to Will. "But it gets you a nice car, huh?" He pointed to the wheels. "What are these rims, twenty inch?"

"They get me where I want to go," Will replied stiffly.

"I'm happy for you, though, *mija*," Lou continued. "Getting off the block." He waved and walked back into his bodega as the light changed and they drove on.

"Sorry," Annie said as she rolled up the window. "He just doesn't like you."

"A lot of people don't like me," Will assured her. "That's kind of why we're doing this." He looked around his seat. "Nash, where's the hand sanitizer?"

"I got rid of it," Annie told him confidently. "It's bad stuff. Creates antibiotic-resistant superbacteria." Then she rifled through her bag until she found an old heart-printed washcloth. She handed it to Will. "Here. Rub real hard."

He shook his head in disgust looking at the grimy washcloth. "I'm good. All right, time for photographs. You ready, Annie?"

Annie smiled up at him. "Let's do this."

# ELEVEN

The next few hours were a whirlwind as Annie and Will posed for pictures in Central Park. Will pushed Annie on the swings, they played soccer, and Will even gave Annie a piggyback ride to go get soft pretzels. Soon, pictures of them were flooding the Internet, going viral in the best possible way.

While Annie was enjoying her pretzel, a reporter approached them. "Annie! Are you having fun?" she called.

"Mr. Stacks is the best!" Annie gushed. "I just wish I was old enough to vote for him."

"That was a bit much," Will told her.

"I'm still finding it." Annie winked.

Later that day, at Guy's suggestion, Will took Annie out for the best photo opportunity yet — adopting a puppy from the local dog shelter. Even the huge gaggle of reporters and camera crews watching couldn't dull Annie's excitement. She'd always wanted a dog.

"How do you choose just one?" Annie asked.

"You don't choose a dog; a dog chooses you," the shelter coordinator told her. She led Annie into a pen filled with dogs.

As soon as Annie stepped inside, the dogs rushed over, jumping on her and licking her.

"They *all* chose me!" she cried, cuddling a tiny puppy.

"Just one," Will said sternly.

Annie played happily with the dogs, trying to find the perfect choice. But she knew she'd found her match when she saw a small sandy-colored dog turning in circles in the corner. It looked just like the dog she'd saved from the boys in the alley. When she looked closer, she realized it *was* the dog she'd saved! The poor little dog was covered in muck and looked like she needed a good meal. As soon as Annie hugged her, she stopped spinning and licked Annie's face. "Hey, girl," Annie cooed. "We found each other. I'll never leave you again. Promise."

"Annie! What are you going to name it?" a reporter asked.

The dog started spinning again, chasing her tail.

"She's like a hurricane," Will said.

"Sandy!" Annie announced. "Her name is going to be Sandy."

Watching from off to the side, Grace pulled up the polls on her phone. Will had shot up — he was only three points behind his opponent!

Just then two girls walked up to Annie.

"Can we take a picture with you?" one of the girls asked.

"Uh, sure," Annie said, looking a little taken aback as they snapped a picture. She wasn't used to being famous.

"You're so cool!" the second girl said, and the girls walked away.

Annie smiled. It felt nice to be noticed.

# TWELVE

That night, Annie climbed into her huge bed with a freshly bathed and groomed Sandy. She was tired, but she was almost afraid to go to sleep. What if she woke up to find the whole wonderful day had been a dream?

Just then her new phone dinged. It was a text from Tessie: *We miss u!* And attached was a photo of all the girls in their room. It dinged again. This time Mia had sent a picture of Miss Hannigan passed out on the sofa. Annie smiled. She took a picture of Sandy with her phone and sent it to them. Then she pulled her locket out from under her nightgown and rubbed it as she lay back against the pillows. She didn't think she'd ever be homesick for Miss Hannigan, but she missed her foster sisters.

She sighed and pushed back the covers. She just wasn't sleepy. Not with all of the day's excitement to think about. She was going to get a snack.

Annie padded down the hall to the kitchen with Sandy beside her. But as she rounded the corner, she was surprised to find Will already in the kitchen. He was sitting at the counter in his pajamas working on his tablet.

"Hey," Annie said.

"Something wrong?" Will asked, barely even looking up.

"Couldn't sleep. It's so quiet here," Annie told him, climbing up onto a stool. "Whatcha doing?"

"Working," Will said.

"This late?" Annie wrinkled her nose.

"Always."

"When do you have fun?" Annie asked, confused.

"This is fun," Will said, looking serious.

"Seems like it," Annie said sarcastically. It sure didn't look fun.

"Are you hungry?" Will asked, changing the subject. "I don't have much here, but I can order in."

"Why don't you have a cook or, like, a million servants?" Annie asked.

"I like to be alone," Will answered.

"So why do you need all this space?"

"I like to be alone in a lot of space," Will said. Annie sure did ask a lot of questions.

"So you can do this and not touch a wall?" Annie hopped up and spun around in circles.

Will watched her and shook his head. "Everybody surrounds themselves with all these people so they feel loved. When really, you can count the people who truly matter on one hand." He held up a closed fist.

"You're making a fist," Annie pointed out. "Where are your people?"

"Not around anymore."

"You don't want new ones?"

"I'm good, thanks," he said firmly.

Annie shrugged. She walked over to the fridge and opened it. It was full of takeout containers.

"I can make a meal out of anything," she said. "Pick five ingredients."

Stacks shook his head.

"Come on," Annie begged. "This'll be fun. Not work, but almost as fun."

Will sighed. "Okay. That fruit, pancetta, I think that's risotto, steak, and the fusilli."

Annie looked at the containers. The only foods she recognized were steak and fruit. But she gathered up the containers anyway and carried them to the stove.

Before starting to cook, she dropped a little bit of the risotto on the floor for Sandy. Then she dumped the rest of the ingredients in a pan. She turned on the heat and stirred and tossed the food — she really looked like she knew what she was doing. Will was impressed in spite of himself; he'd never cooked anything.

When she was finished, she spooned her concoction onto two plates and slid one in front of Will. He took a bite and immediately spit it out. It was horrible.

Annie laughed. "It's gross. Sorry. But you've got to learn to stop spitting. You're not a camel."

Will finally smiled. "I have a movie premiere tomorrow. Guy thinks you should come."

Annie nodded eagerly. "Guy's right!" She couldn't remember the last time she'd been to a movie — her or her foster sisters. "Can I bring my friends?" she asked.

"There are *more* of you?" Will asked incredulously.

"More photos!" Annie reminded him.

After eating a leftover piece of pizza Annie found in one of the takeout containers, she went back to bed. But she still couldn't sleep. The room was just too big and empty. It felt lonely. Finally she got up and went into the walk-in closet. That felt better.

She pulled her comforter and pillow inside the closet and lay down with Sandy next to her. There, she finally slept.

# THIRTEEN

The next morning, Annie pulled Nash aside before they all headed out. "I know this sounds crazy, but do you guys spy on people with your phones?"

"Why?" he asked.

"I really need to find some people," she said, giving him her best puppy-dog eyes.

There was no way he could say no to that. So he took Annie downstairs to the Stacks Mobile control room in the bottom of the building. Screens showing maps of the city covered every wall and each map was covered in tiny glowing dots — one for each Stacks phone being used.

On side screens, texts, pictures, tweets, and websites scrolled constantly, showing what users were accessing in each area.

"Welcome to the Stacks Mobile control center," Nash said as they walked in. "We can trace every call and data transmission made on every carrier for the past twenty years." He took a look at Annie's jaw hanging open and laughed. "People shouldn't be scared of the government, they should be scared of cell-phone companies."

"Lou was right," Annie murmured to herself. Then she turned back to Nash. "Can you use all this to search for my parents?"

"Bennett, right?" Nash asked. Annie nodded and Nash walked over to a map. He zoomed in until little names popped up over the dots.

"Can you go back five years? Around the Twenty-Sixth Precinct?" Annie asked hopefully. "That's where they left me."

Nash turned and looked at her. She seemed so hopeful it almost broke his heart. "It'll take a bit. I'll let you know," Nash said kindly, putting his arm around her shoulder.

"Thanks," Annie said.

That afternoon, Annie went to her very first movie premiere. Will, Guy, and Grace took Annie, Tessie, Isabella, Pepper, and Mia. They all got dressed up in their most fashionable outfits to walk the red carpet, and the girls had a great time striking silly poses for the media, although the reporters only had eyes for Annie.

"Who are you wearing?" one asked.

"This is my friend Isabella's." Annie pointed to her skirt. "And this I found somewhere!" She showed off her top.

"Did you like the French toast you had for breakfast this morning?" another reporter shouted out.

"It was so good." Annie smiled. Then she paused. "Wait, how'd you know that?"

"You tweeted it; @Annie4Realz," he told her, looking as if she ought to have already known that.

"We made you a Twitter account. You already have three million followers," Guy explained. "Get it? Annie, 4, Realz, with a Z. Because you keep it *realz*."

Annie rolled her eyes. Guy tried way too hard to be cool sometimes.

Just then Will walked past, heading back to the SUV.

"Where are you going?" Annie called after him.

"Back to work," he answered over his shoulder.

"No one stays for the movie," Grace explained as she, too, headed for the car. "We just walk the red carpet to get the press. It's all for show."

"But I invited my friends," Annie said, looking stricken. "Can't we stay and see the movie?"

Will shrugged. "Sure. Go ahead." Then he continued on his way, but a reporter noticed and ran after him.

"Aren't you staying with Annie?" the reporter asked loudly, catching the attention of all of the other reporters.

Will froze in place. More and more reporters started running over. He couldn't escape now. So he turned back around with a big smile on his face. "Just forgot my phone!" He walked back up the red carpet toward Annie and grabbed Grace's arm as he went, whispering to her, "You're coming with me. Make sure I don't kill anyone."

Annie and her friends couldn't contain their excitement as the movie started. It was based on a bestselling teen book and featured the hottest young actors in Hollywood! Will, on the other hand, was having trouble keeping up with the plot. Luckily, he was sitting next to Annie, and she was more than happy to explain it to him. Before long he was as engrossed as the girls. By the end, he and Annie were both yelling at the screen and cheering loudly during the final battle scene. Grace couldn't help smiling when she saw him bonding with Annie over the cheesy film.

This was a side of Will Stacks she had never seen before. And it was coming out because of Annie.

The girls and Will discussed the movie all the way out of the theater.

"I want to be Saffron so bad!" Isabella groaned, looking at a poster of the pretty actress.

"I can't believe Sakana told on them." Tessie grinned, pointing to another character on the poster.

Annie is a foster child in Harlem. She always believes the sun'll come out tomorrow!

Annie lives with her foster sisters in mean, old Miss Hannigan's apartment. It's the hard-knock life!

**Will Stacks is a billionaire who is running to be the mayor of New York City.**

**Will saves Annie from being hit by a car!**

**Guy convinces Will to have Annie
stay with him to boost his campaign image.**

Annie has never been in such a huge home before!

Annie and Will put on quite the show for the press.

**Grace wonders if Annie might just be
the family Will needs in his life.**

**Annie loves her adopted dog, Sandy . . .**

. . . and the press loves Annie!

**Annie helps Will at a campaign fund-raiser.**

**Guy has a sneaky idea to boost
Will's campaign chances.**

Annie gives Will a homemade card to say good-bye.

Will Annie find her true family after all?

"Of course she did," Will explained. "You can't trust the fish people. Gwarklark warned them."

"I think she was bluffing," Grace added.

"Nope, it was a warning," Pepper said matter-of-factly. "They come back in the next movie."

"There's a next movie?!" Will exclaimed.

Annie nodded. "There are four more."

"Shut up!" Will cried. He playfully shoved Annie and then picked her up and twirled her around. She giggled as he threw her in the air. But then his phone rang and he put her down gently. He looked at the screen and sighed. "I've got to go."

The girls all thanked him for letting them come to the movie.

"Can't we stay for the party?" Annie begged.

Will looked at his phone again. "I haven't worked in two hours. Three of my guys think I'm dead."

"You've worked enough," Annie persuaded him. "If your building gets any taller, it's going to hit the sun."

Will laughed. "You have this crazy way of turning nos into yeses. What is that?"

"I think when people say no, they're really just scared of saying yes," Annie said with a smile.

Will looked over at Grace, but she just held her hands up and smiled. "Don't look at me. This is all you."

He looked from Annie to his phone and back at Annie. "I guess it couldn't hurt . . ."

The girls squealed with excitement. Annie grabbed Will's hand and dragged him into the after-premiere party.

The hall was decorated with tons of movie merchandise and was filled with amazing activity areas — a buffet, a candy bar, a create-your-own-jewelry stand, a makeover booth, and even a small indoor ice-skating rink. It was incredible!

The girls ran from area to area, picking up swag bags and trying out new jewelry.

But it wasn't long before Will really did have to go. Guy came to collect him for another obligation. "We're late for the Jets-Giants game. You need to flip the ceremonial coin. They're both New York teams, so heads or tails, you need to be equally happy and sad."

"Go ahead. I'll take them back," Grace assured him. Then she smiled. "This was kind of fun."

"Yeah," Will said, looking over at Annie playing a video game. This had been fun. He turned to go but Annie ran after him.

"Mr. Stacks!" she called. "You forgot your goody bag." She handed him a sparkly bag filled with movie merchandise. He put it over his shoulder and left, smiling.

A few hours later, Grace and Annie dropped the girls back off at Miss Hannigan's apartment. As she watched her friends shimmy up the fire escape, Annie turned to Grace and asked, "Can we make one stop?"

# FOURTEEN

The girls snuck back up to their room, shut the door, turned their music on low, and then danced around playing with their swag and talking about the premiere. They tried to be quiet, but they were just too excited, and they woke up Miss Hannigan.

"Why are you still up?" she shouted, throwing their door open. "Where'd you get all this stuff?!"

The girls went silent. But Miss Hannigan knew just how to get them to talk. She went down the line, glaring at each girl until finally Tessie broke. "We went with Annie to a movie and then got candy and soda and went ice-skating and Mr. Stacks is so cool and I got fish earrings," she said breathlessly.

"Nice, Tessie," Pepper hissed.

"I can't keep a secret!" Tessie wailed.

"Annie got you all this?" Miss Hannigan said coldly. An icy glare came to her eyes. "Well, you don't have to keep this a secret: Pack it up. It's going back."

"Why?" Isabella asked in disbelief.

"Because you don't deserve it. And neither does Annie. She's not your friend. And neither is *Mister* Stacks. They're all just parasites who suck the life out of you, then move on when you're not the shiny object anymore. No one cares about you. You rats need to start realizing that," Miss Hannigan said cruelly.

"You're being mean!" Mia cried, tears already streaming down her face.

"I'm being educational. I used to be a dopey little girl like you. Now, pack up this stuff," Miss Hannigan bellowed and then marched out, slamming the door behind her.

She stomped down the hall and plopped on the sofa, only to hear Annie's name on the radio. She reached over and turned it up.

"The city's most-famous girl, Annie, was spotted today at a movie premiere, and we got to talk to her," the DJ said. "So, Annie, did you like the movie?"

"It was so good! And the song was great!" Annie exclaimed, then she sang, *"All over the world we're singing, na na na na na na na na!"*

"Not only is she smart and cute, sounds like she can really sing. Not long before she gets a record contract," the DJ finished.

Miss Hannigan screamed into a pillow and then threw it at the radio, knocking it to the floor.

It just wasn't fair! That little brat was out living the life Miss Hannigan had always wanted and she *definitely* didn't deserve it. There had to be a way for Miss Hannigan to get a piece of Annie's newfound fame.

She just had to figure out how.

Later that evening, Annie and Grace sat outside of Domani on the curb, both of them writing their names in sidewalk chalk as they talked.

"You come here every Friday?" Grace asked.

Annie nodded. "It's the only day they serve cannoli."

"That's all you have to go on? Do you remember what they look like?" Grace asked.

"I think I'll just know," Annie said quietly, grasping her locket.

A few minutes later the restaurant closed for the night. Annie's favorite waiter came out with two take-out boxes. "Cannoli," he told them as he handed them the boxes. "And one for your pretty friend."

Annie sighed. It had been another wasted night. When she looked up, Grace was watching her closely, looking concerned.

"Don't worry," Annie said. "I'll be okay. But can you not tell Mr. Stacks? I don't want to bother him with it."

"Sure," Grace said. Then she pulled Annie into a hug and took her home to Will's apartment.

Will and Guy had been working since the moment they arrived at the penthouse, strategizing on how to get Will further up in the polls. They'd watched interview after interview of his opponent, Harold Gray, and they were running out of ideas.

"Uh-oh," Guy said, pointing to the television, "this looks bad."

A commercial for Will's opponent had just come on, featuring a famous actor.

"He's worked selflessly his entire life for New York. From his first job teaching in inner-city schools to his twenty-five-year stint on the city council, all the while working as a volunteer EMT, Harold Gray is the only *honest* choice for mayor," the actor said.

Harold, Will Stacks's opponent in the race for mayor, came on the screen. "As mayor I will do everything that's right for the *people* of New York, not the *business* of New York."

Guy grimaced. "You've plateaued." He held up his tablet to show Will the data. Will was three points behind Harold and had been for a week. "Annie's gotten you here, but I think this is as far as she'll take you. But it's not over yet. How bad do you want this? How far are you willing to go? Or should I say, how far do you want me to go?"

"I pay you a lot of money not to ask questions like that," Will replied.

"Got it." Guy nodded just as Annie and Grace arrived.

"We're back," Grace called.

Annie ran over to Will and handed him her take-out box. "I brought you a cannoli."

"Because you're an Italian grandmother." Will laughed. "Makes perfect sense."

Annie laughed, too.

"We have a charity event tomorrow," Guy reminded Will. "You should go to bed."

"Okay, G-Money. Keep your shirt on," Annie joked. Then she called Sandy over and went on to bed.

"Did she just sass me?" Guy asked. "What kind of kid are you raising here?"

"A smart one," Grace quipped.

Will headed to his room an hour later. He peeked in to check on Annie, but she wasn't in her bed. He walked into her room and looked around, starting to panic until he heard snoring. It was coming from the closet.

"Annie?" he called. He pushed the closet door open and found Annie asleep on the floor with Sandy curled up next to her.

He sighed. No kid should have to deal with all the things Annie had been through in her ten short years.

# FIFTEEN

The next morning, Will decided to take Annie on an adventure. He found her eating breakfast at the counter. "Morning." He grinned at her.

"Made you breakfast," Annie said, smiling. Then she pointed to a plate of slightly greenish eggs.

"What are you doing today?" Will asked, picking up the plate. "Thought it might be fun to come to work with me."

"Cool!" Annie exclaimed. "I'll go change. Don't let your food get cold."

"No, ma'am. Looks great," he assured her, but as soon as she went to her room, Will put the plate down on the floor for Sandy to eat. There was no way he was touching that food! Sandy came over, sniffed the eggs, and then turned around and sat on them.

"Do you get airsick?" Will asked as he helped Annie climb up into his private helicopter.

"Don't know. I've never been in the air," Annie said cheerfully, then added, "I threw up on the swings once."

Will handed her a throw-up bag — just in case. Then he said, "We're doing a cell tower check. To make sure they're all working."

"*You* do that yourself?" Annie asked as they rose up into the air and headed out over Manhattan.

"I told you work is fun." Will smiled. "You want to know the secret to Never Drop A Call?"

"Sure," Annie said eagerly.

"We have five times as many cell towers as the other guys. But we hide them in plain sight. Like right there." Will pointed at the Statue of Liberty right in front of them. "Do you see it? It's on her crown."

Annie craned her neck, but she couldn't spot the tower. "No."

"Exactly," Will said with a smile and held up his hand. Annie gave him a high five.

Next they flew over the Brooklyn Bridge.

"See them? They're on every wire." Will pointed out the cell towers.

"That's so cool. How'd you do this? How'd you become king of the world?" Annie asked in awe.

"Worked my butt off," Will said. "The harder I worked, the more opportunities I got. You've got to play with the cards you've been dealt. Even if they're bad."

"What if you haven't got any cards?" Annie asked.

"Then you bluff." Will gestured out the window. "That's why I love this city. It doesn't care who or what you are. Just if you want it bad enough. And what you do with what you've got."

"I see a cell tower!" Annie exclaimed.

"Where?" Will asked, craning his neck to see.

"On that building. See it? Right there." Annie pointed to an office building.

"There it is." Will nodded. He watched as Annie continued looking out at the view and he smiled to himself. "Sometimes what you're looking for is right in front of your face."

# SIXTEEN

That evening, Annie was going with Will to a gala at the Guggenheim Museum. Will had been getting ready for an hour, but Annie was waiting for Grace to arrive. Annie walked past the bathroom where Will was washing his face and caught a glimpse of something that made her gasp.

Will was completely bald! A wig of his normal, perfectly cut hair was resting on a mannequin head next to the sink.

Annie hurried away before he could see her, but she couldn't stop smiling. Who would have ever imagined that billionaire Will Stacks was bald?

A few minutes later, Will came out wearing his tuxedo, his hair styled as usual.

"Hey, Annie," he said slowly. "Did you just see . . . ?"

"I didn't see anything." Annie pretended to be playing with Sandy and didn't look up.

"Because I thought I saw you in the . . ." Will continued, rubbing his neck.

"Nope. Here the whole time," Annie said.

Just then the elevator doors slid open and Grace walked in, dressed to the nines in a gown and heels.

"Wow." Will whistled as soon as he saw her, almost at a loss for words. "You look . . ."

Grace blushed. "So do you," she said shyly.

Annie glanced back and forth between Will and Grace. A huge grin crossed her face. It was totally obvious that Will and Grace liked each other! Well, maybe obvious to everyone *except* Will and Grace.

Finally Grace broke Will's gaze and turned to Annie. "Let's go get you dressed."

A short while later, Grace waited while Annie changed into her charity event outfit.

"Ready?" Annie called from the closet.

"Very excited," Grace called back.

Annie opened the closet door and emerged wearing

an adorable red dress. She walked over to the mirror and smiled at her reflection.

"It's gorgeous," Grace said. "You're gorgeous,"

"I can't believe it," Annie said in awe. She slid her locket around her neck, playing with it.

Will knocked on the door and walked in. "Let's go! We're going to be late." Then he stopped mid-step when he caught sight of Annie. "Wow. Annie."

"I know, right?" Annie said happily.

"Get out of here; we're not done," Grace said, shooing him out.

"When did this stop being my house?" Will asked, shaking his head at the two girls before heading out to wait in the living room.

Annie sat down in front of Grace so that Grace could do her hair. "Why aren't you and Mr. Stacks together?" Annie asked innocently.

Grace paused, surprised. "Well, that's a complicated question."

"Not really," Annie said matter-of-factly. "Do you like him?"

"I work for him," Grace pointed out. "Liking him doesn't come into play. I'm too busy working to bother with anything else."

"That sounds like something Mr. Stacks would say," Annie told her. "When my friend Pepper liked this boy at school, she punched him in the face. She got suspended, but they play in the park together now. Maybe you should try that with Mr. Stacks."

Grace couldn't help smiling. Annie certainly had a unique way of looking at the world. She doubted punching Mr. Stacks was the right way to go about things. Still, perhaps Annie did have a point. "He is very good-looking," Grace mused. "Great chiseled face. Good hair."

Annie giggled. "I wouldn't bank on the hair, sister."

# SEVENTEEN

An hour later, Will, Annie, and Grace walked the red carpet at the Guggenheim gala with Nash and Guy trailing behind them. They did short interviews and posed for pictures until they reached the museum president.

"Thanks for doing this, Will," the president said, shaking Will's hand. "Your name's going to look great up there."

"Are you sure the Guggenheims are okay with this?" Will asked in a low voice.

"You gave me a hundred million reasons not to care," the president assured him.

Bored with the financial talk, Annie turned to Nash. "Did they find anything on my parents?"

"Not yet," he told her. "And they dug pretty deep. Sorry."

Annie's face fell. "Thanks for trying," she said sincerely. But she looked disappointed.

"You're going to find your family, Annie. I promise," Nash assured her.

As they were talking, neither Annie nor Nash noticed Guy listening in on their conversation.

Will gave a rousing speech to the crowd at the gala while Annie enjoyed plate after plate of delicious grilled shrimp. "These are ridiculous!" she told Grace happily, stuffing an oversized shrimp into her mouth.

". . . New Yorkers face many challenges every day, challenges that seem insurmountable," Will was saying. "We all tell ourselves no a lot. 'No, I won't get that job.' 'No, I can't afford college.' 'No, no, no.' Well, it's time to turn the nos into yeses. Because when we say no, we're really just scared of the yes. So say yes to yourselves and say yes to a brighter life." Will paused for applause and then continued, "Many of you know I've had a visitor staying with me recently. She only knows the word *yes*."

A spotlight came to rest on Annie, with her mouth full of shrimp. There was more applause as she smiled and waved, frantically swallowing.

"Annie, can you come up here? We all know you're not shy." Will gestured to Annie and she walked up to the podium amid light laughter. "I don't want to embarrass you, I just want everyone to see what the future of this city is all about. Do you have anything to say to these good people, oozing with generous guilt?"

Everyone laughed again, even Annie. Then she took the microphone. "I can't believe I'm here. In a dress that feels like a cloud. Standing in the middle of a giant cinnamon roll. With a band that has little violins, big violins . . . Ooh, a triangle! I've played that. That's a real thing? One of those, another one of those. It's such a big opportunity."

Guy stepped forward and whispered to Annie, "Read your speech."

"What?" she whispered back, looking startled.

"I wrote you a speech. It's right there on the teleprompter," Guy replied.

Annie looked at the teleprompter and shook her head. "I don't want to."

"Are you all right?" Will asked, realizing Annie suddenly seemed upset.

"Just read it! It's right there," Guy urged.

"Is it too far away?" Will asked, wanting to help.

"I'll make it bigger," Guy offered.

Annie looked back and forth between them and then burst into tears. "No! Leave me alone!" she yelled and then ran off the stage and out of the museum.

Will, Grace, and Guy followed Annie as fast as they could, but it took them almost an entire block to catch up to her.

"Annie!" Will called out as he grabbed hold of her shoulder and pulled her to him.

"I did the interviews and took the pictures and came up on stage — wasn't that enough?" Annie said through sobs.

Will crouched down so he was at Annie's eye level. "Are we asking you to do too much?"

Annie just shook her head, tears falling fast.

"What's wrong?" Will asked kindly. But that just made Annie cry harder. "Tell me right now, Annie. You've got to tell me."

"No, I don't." Annie sniffed. "You're not my dad."

Will pulled back a little. That stung. But still, he couldn't leave Annie. Not when she really needed him. "Didn't say I was," he said softly. "Now what's wrong? I'm not leaving here until you tell me."

Annie shook her head. But finally she said quietly, "I can't read."

"What?" Will was confused. "I've seen you read."

Annie shook her head again. "Sorry I ruined your shrimp event."

A flash went off as the photographers from the gala found them and started taking pictures.

"No pictures!" Will said forcefully, holding his hand in front of Annie's face. "She's a little girl! And she's upset!"

Will used his jacket to shield Annie and hurried her and Grace into the SUV. As Guy and Nash followed, Guy asked, "What was she talking to you about earlier, Nash?"

"Asked us to find her parents. But it's a dead end. I

even called my old buddies on the force. There's nothing on that kid," Nash said, looking sad. "Poor Annie."

Guy's eyebrows shot up. "That's genius," he said to himself. Then he took off in the other direction with his phone out.

# EIGHTEEN

Thirty minutes later, Guy buzzed the intercom in front of Miss Hannigan's apartment.

"Who is it?" Miss Hannigan asked through the speaker.

"Guy Danlily," Guy answered. "I work for Will Stacks."

Miss Hannigan looked out the window at the door. When she saw handsome Guy in his tuxedo, she buzzed him up right away and then hurried to change into a dress and touch up her makeup.

By the time Guy knocked on the door, Miss Hannigan was waiting breathlessly to open it. "Hello there," she purred.

"Colleen Hannigan?" Guy asked.

Miss Hannigan giggled. "My maiden name. But I'm not married to it. If you know what I mean."

"Sorry to bother you so late," Guy said. "But can I . . . buy you dinner?"

Miss Hannigan reached out to take his arm. Those were the sweetest words in the English language.

Guy took Miss Hannigan to a jazz club. They sat at a small table where they could talk, although Miss Hannigan was more interested in flirting than talking. But Guy was all business.

"I want to talk to you about Annie," he said.

"*Ugh,*" Miss Hannigan groaned. "Of course you do."

"What do you know about her parents?" Guy asked. "Any and all details."

Miss Hannigan glared at him. "What's your game, dude?"

"What?" Guy asked innocently.

"I know who you are," she told him. "You're that

guy in all the photos lurking in the background, pulling strings, cleaning up messes."

Guy looked offended. "I don't lurk."

She raised an eyebrow at him, and then asked, "So what is this? Are you pulling, or are you cleaning?"

Guy looked at her carefully. "If Will wins this race for mayor," he said, "I get paid a fortune. More than anything I've ever made, combined."

That got Miss Hannigan's attention. "Why so much?" she asked.

Guy shrugged. "It's like getting paid long odds on a dark horse. Do you know how hard it is to get Will Stacks elected?"

"There have been worse politicians," Miss Hannigan pointed out.

"I know. I've gotten them elected," Guy told her. "But I'm over it. Over being the cockroach everyone needs but treats like . . ."

"A cockroach?" Miss Hannigan finished.

"Exactly. This is my last roll at the table. Get paid and I'm out."

"There's no such thing as a way out," Miss Hannigan said with a bitter little laugh. "Trust me."

"There's always a way out," Guy countered. "Trust *me*. And in this particular case, it's all about finding Annie's parents."

"They don't exist," Miss Hannigan told him. "That little brat has no one, and somehow she still ended up on top, while I'm stuck down in the gutter."

"We can make them exist," Will assured her. "Get two people to pretend to be her parents. They'll know every detail and miraculously show up right before the election. Add water, instant parents! I'll find the parents. I just need details from you — everything you know about Annie. Anything that a parent would know. Any secrets she has."

Miss Hannigan thought for a moment and then nodded. It could work. But she wasn't about to give up the information she knew for free.

"What's in it for me?" she asked slyly. "Other than seeing Annie get what she deserves?"

"Same as me," Guy assured her. "Money. And no more being the cockroach."

"I knew I liked you," Miss Hannigan said with a smile.

Guy raised his drink. "To a way out. To easy street." They clinked glasses.

Meanwhile, back at the penthouse, Will walked into the living room. He had just tucked Annie into bed.

Will looked at Grace and shook his head. "I've been telling her she can do anything she wants in this city, but we haven't even taught her to read. How does this happen?"

"A lot of kids get lost, Will," Grace said gently. "A lot of people get lost."

"That's unacceptable," Will said, slamming his fist down on the table. "We've got to get her a tutor."

"For *her*, though, right?" Grace asked. "Not just for the press."

"Of course for her," Will said. Grace smiled, and that caught Will off guard. "What?" he asked.

"Your secret's safe with me," she told him. "You know, that you care."

"About kids in New York? Yeah, I care," Will said.

Grace took his hand. "And Annie."

# NINETEEN

The next morning, Annie packed her bag and took Sandy to the kitchen to say good-bye to Will.

"Where are you going?" Will asked when he saw her bag. He didn't understand what she was doing.

"Thanks for everything," Annie told him. "Sorry I messed up last night. Hope it doesn't hurt your chances too bad."

Will was completely confused. "What are you talking about?"

"It's okay. I'm good at this part. I've had a lot of practice leaving places," Annie assured him.

Will shook his head. "Put your bag down. You're not going anywhere," he said firmly.

"Sandy's gotta go," Annie said.

"Stop it. You're both staying. I don't care what happened." Will put his hand on her shoulder.

"No," Annie insisted. "I mean, Sandy's *gotta go*."

She nodded down toward the little dog, who looked like she was about to burst.

"All right," Will said. "Then let's take Sandy out, together."

Annie and Will went down to the street and walked along the block, letting Sandy sniff wherever she wanted.

"So you can't read," Will prompted "But I saw you sign your name."

"That's all you've got to know how to do," Annie replied.

"None of your teachers know? How is that possible?" Will asked.

"I'm good at hiding it."

"What about at home? Didn't anyone catch it?" Will pushed.

"At home?" Annie scoffed. "Are you crazy? Miss Hannigan never cared about that stuff." Just then a bus went by. "Let me show you how I do it," Annie said. She pointed to the bus. "That's an uptown bus. You can tell by the numbers." She pointed across the street. "That's a pizza place. And that's an ad of you running for mayor.

"I listen to the news," Annie continued. "'It's going to rain today and hand sanitizer is bad for you and Will Stacks is sinking in the polls.' So people think I'm smart."

Will took Annie's shoulders. "You *are* smart. It won't take you long to learn to read. I'm getting you a tutor."

"It's okay, I don't —"

Will cut her off. "Let me help you. Why didn't you tell anybody?"

Annie snorted. "It's not like the whole world wants a foster kid to begin with."

"You could've told me. Or Grace," Will said gently.

Annie shrugged and looked down at her feet. "Didn't know what you would've done with me."

Will couldn't bear to see her so hurt. "Let's go," he said, taking her hand and pulling her toward where Nash had the company car parked. "I want to show you something."

Nash drove Annie and Will up to the Bronx, where Will grew up.

"Thanks, Nash. We'll find our way back," Will said as he and Annie got out of the SUV.

Nash waved and drove away. Will led Annie down the sidewalk. "Everybody's got something they don't want other people to know. Including me," he told her. They turned a corner and were standing beneath an overpass. "This is it. My family."

Annie looked around. There was no one there. She looked around again . . . and then up at Will. "Uh . . . can *you* see them right now?" she asked.

"In my head," Will answered. "My dad built this section of the track. Worked twenty hours a day. He died when I was twelve."

"What was he like?" Annie asked, curious.

"Barely saw him," Will told her. "He was always working."

"What about your mom?" Annie asked.

"Never knew her. I lived with my grandma when my dad died."

Annie thought for a moment. Will wasn't so different from her. He didn't really know his parents either. But he did know one thing about his father: He had worked hard all his life. "That's why you work so hard?" she asked. "Because he did?"

Will nodded and then made a fist with his hand and held it up for Annie to see. "But I think that's also why I got this."

By holding up his fist, Will meant that he had gotten his strength by working hard like his father. But Annie could tell it also meant he thought he was on his own. No people to count on. Just himself.

"That's what you don't want people to know?" she asked.

Will nodded.

Annie reached out and put one of his fingers up. "Let me help you. I'll be one of your people."

Will and Annie spent the rest of the day hanging out in the Bronx. They went to play ball in the park. Will pushed Annie on the swings. And they ate hot dogs from a street cart — all with no photographers in sight.

Annie fell asleep on the subway car and Will

carried her the rest of the way home. Back at the penthouse, he tucked Annie into bed.

As he left her room, Will couldn't help thinking about how much his life had changed in just the past few days. How much he had changed. All this time, he had believed that if he ran for mayor, if he grew his company even larger, then he would feel fulfilled. That maybe, somehow, his father would be proud.

But there was a little sleeping girl in that room who was already proud of him. Even more than that, she needed him. And that made Will Stacks feel fulfilled.

Will quietly closed the door to Annie's room. Then he pulled out his cell phone and called Grace.

"Let me ask you something," he said. "How hard is it to become a foster parent? I don't mean temporarily, I mean, like a permanent situation."

"You mean adopt her?" Grace asked.

"Whatever the word is." Will nodded.

"That's the word," Grace assured him.

"Then let's do that," Will said with a smile.

# TWENTY

Annie had her first meeting with her tutor the next day in Will's conference room. While Annie practiced with the tutor, Will and Grace worked in the room next door.

Will tried to focus on work, but he kept getting up to peer through the glass conference room windows and see how Annie was doing.

"It's only been two hours," Grace teased him. "I don't think she's completely learned how to read yet."

Suddenly, Guy burst into the room. "We got our game-changer!" Guy announced excitedly. "Every election needs a game-changer, and we got our game-changer."

"Stop saying game-changer." Grace rolled her eyes.

"Well, whether I say it or not, Annie's parents are ours," Guy told Will, handing him a file. "They saw a picture of Annie and called us. It's a miracle!"

Will and Grace exchanged an astonished look.

"They've been trying to find her for years but there's nothing in the system," Guy continued.

"How do they know she's their daughter?" Grace asked.

"They know everything about her — the note, the locket . . . and, oh yeah, I ran a DNA test," Guy explained with a smile.

Will flipped through the papers in the file. He was shocked. He knew he should be happy for Annie, but he didn't want to let her go. Not now, after he had just decided he wanted to be her father. "I want to meet them first. Before Annie finds out," Will told Guy firmly.

Guy could see Annie standing in the doorway, although Will couldn't. "I wouldn't have it any other way. You should totally be the one who tells Annie we found her parents," Guy said loudly enough for Annie to hear.

"You found my parents?!" Annie exclaimed, running into the room.

Will glared at Guy, but Guy just shrugged, playing innocent.

"Yes, honey. I think so," Grace said gently.

"No way! Really?" she cried.

Will had never seen Annie so excited.

"We're meeting them this afternoon," Guy told her enthusiastically. "At this place called . . . Domani?"

"That's where the note is from! I knew they'd come for me! I told you I'd find my family!" Annie cheered. She couldn't contain her excitement.

"I'm happy for you, Annie," Will said kindly, trying to hide how crushed he was.

"It's all because of you." Annie hugged Will as hard as she could. "I found my real parents!"

A few hours later, when they arrived at Domani, there were huge crowds of reporters and photographers waiting outside.

"Why are they all here?" Annie asked nervously. She didn't really want this first meeting on camera.

"I said no press until after it's confirmed," Will said harshly, looking from Guy to Grace to Nash.

"This isn't me," Guy lied. "Someone must've leaked it. Grace?"

"Say my name again," Grace threatened him. "Will, you know it wasn't me."

"I don't get why everyone wants to be famous," Annie muttered.

"They think it means people like them," Will explained.

Will and his team led Annie into the restaurant and back to where her parents and Ms. Kovacevic were waiting. The man and woman stood up, and Annie gazed at her parents for the first time.

After so many years of waiting, so many years of longing to meet them, Annie wasn't quite sure how to feel. Her father had smooth dark skin. And her mother had pretty braided hair. Neither of them quite resembled Annie, or perhaps what Annie had always imagined they would look like. But then again, Annie only had her imagination to compare them to. Seeing them in person for the first time somehow made Annie feel anxious and nervous and awkward all at once.

Of course, only Guy and Miss Hannigan knew that Annie's "parents" were really actors, paid to play the part.

Annie's favorite waiter came over and pulled out a chair so Annie could sit down. "I'm very happy for you," he told her. She smiled up at him. Then Annie's "parents" rushed forward to hug her.

"Annie!" her dad exclaimed.

"My girl!" Her mom pulled Annie in close. Then she revealed a locket from under her collar that was a perfect match to the locket Annie always wore. "We thought we had lost you forever."

"Me, too," Annie said. She couldn't believe this was really, finally happening.

"We were going through some tough times and thought it would be best if someone else looked after you," her dad explained.

"I've never forgiven myself for it," her mom said, looking choked up. "When we got back on our feet we couldn't find you. But the angels were looking out."

Off to the side, Miss Hannigan approached Will while Annie was telling her parents about her school. "Hi. Remember me? From before?"

Will grimaced. "Sorry about that. I didn't realize you were Annie's foster mom."

"Among other things," Miss Hannigan said flirtatiously.

"She said you have a great voice," Will told her kindly.

"She did?" Miss Hannigan asked, taken aback. She never thought Annie would compliment her.

"You do," Annie assured her, having caught the end of Will and Miss Hannigan's conversation.

"I loved C+C Music Factory," Will volunteered.

"Should we get started?" Guy asked. Before anyone could answer, he brought Ms. Kovacevic over to help them fill out the forms to turn Annie back over to her mom and dad.

Ms. Kovacevic skimmed through the papers. "Everything is in order, DNA test; the judge signed it. We just need signatures from the parents."

Annie's mom and dad both signed while Will pulled Guy aside.

"Are we sure about this?" Will asked. He had a bad feeling about Annie's "parents." Something felt off.

"That this is going to win you the election?" Guy asked. "Yeah. Game-changer!"

"No, I mean Annie," Will insisted.

"You don't pay me to worry about her," Guy replied.

Just then Ms. Kovacevic called Will over to sign as the temporary guardian. Will looked at Annie. Annie smiled at him, nodding encouragingly, and that made Will feel better. He signed.

"According to the state of New York, you are officially reunited," Ms. Kovacevic announced.

"Hooray!" Guy cheered.

"Where do you live?" Annie asked her parents.

"New Jersey," her mom said.

Annie cringed.

"But we're moving to Brazil for my job," her dad added.

"I think you're going to like it there," her mom said, brushing some hair from Annie's face.

Annie suddenly felt a shiver run through her. These were her parents . . . but somehow it didn't feel quite right. Or at least the way she had always imagined it.

"Can I go back with Mr. Stacks? To say good-bye?" Annie asked.

"Sure," her mom said. "We'll pick you up at four."

Annie looked back at Will. He looked kindly at her, but Annie could tell he was a little sad, too.

Annie didn't understand. This was what she had always wanted.

So why did it feel so weird?

Miss Hannigan pulled Guy aside on the way out. "How'd you do the DNA test?" she asked in a harsh whisper.

"You can do anything with money." Guy chuckled.

Miss Hannigan looked over at Annie. It was true, the little brat annoyed her more than anyone. But now that this was all actually happening, Miss Hannigan suddenly wondered what *exactly* would happen to Annie.

"Who are those people? What's your plan with her?" she hissed.

"Doesn't matter. She served her purpose," Guy replied, uninterested.

"What does that mean?" Miss Hannigan asked sharply.

Guy sighed. "They'll hold her for a while, then dump her back into the system after the election. No harm, no foul," Guy assured her.

Miss Hannigan looked shocked. "Sounds like a lot of harm. You can't do that. She's still a little girl."

"Why do you care?" Guy was beginning to get

annoyed. "You did your part and you'll get your money. Just go home and keep your mouth shut."

"You can't talk to me like that," Miss Hannigan told him. "I know things."

Guy stepped forward so that he was right in her face. "Then if you know what's good for you, you'll go home and keep your mouth shut." He gave her a warning look that caused Miss Hannigan to shrink back. Then Guy turned and followed Will and Annie out into the sea of reporters.

Miss Hannigan stood there with her mouth open. This had gone too far. This wasn't what she wanted.

She had made a horrible mistake.

# TWENTY-ONE

Miss Hannigan stopped at Lou's bodega on the way home to buy a diet soda and a lottery ticket. The television was on behind the counter and she could see the report from earlier with Will and Annie, looking scared and anxious, standing with Annie's fake parents.

"Hey, baby. Haven't seen you in here for a while. How you doing?" Lou asked.

"Not good," Miss Hannigan admitted.

"You want me to make you a sandwich? Roast beef?" Lou asked, concerned.

Miss Hannigan paused. She needed advice. "You

ever do something you think is a good idea at the time, but then after, you're not so sure?" Miss Hannigan asked.

"Three ex-wives. Yes, yes, and *sí*." Lou laughed. "What happened? Whatever you did, you know I'll help."

Miss Hannigan really looked at him, as if seeing him for the first time. "Why are you so nice to me, with the way I treat you?"

"Because under all that bitter, there's a sweet lady with a big heart. She's just been gone for a while," Lou told her.

"Well." Miss Hannigan took a deep breath. "I need your help."

Annie video-chatted with her foster sisters from Will's kitchen when she got home. She wanted to say good-bye in person, but there wasn't enough time.

The girls couldn't wait to hear all about Annie's parents. After all, finding them was a dream come true!

"What are your parents like?" Mia asked. "Are they what you imagined?"

"They seem cool, I guess." Annie shrugged. "Not really what I pictured."

"We'll miss you," Isabella said. "Come visit, okay?"

"Of course. You're my sisters," Annie said.

"We've got to go," Tessie said suddenly.

"Miss Hannigan's coming," Pepper added.

"Bye!" Annie said, touching the screen fondly as the call ended.

"Do you want something to eat?" Will asked Annie after the screen went dark. He'd seen how sad she looked on the call.

"Always," Annie said, managing a small smile.

"My turn to cook," he told her. He pulled takeout containers out of the fridge and let her choose five ingredients.

"That stuff, that, whatever that is, that liquidy thing, and that goo," Annie said, pointing out her choices.

Will sniffed the last one. "I think that's mold, but it's all good."

Will did his best to cook, but he was as hopeless as Annie. By the time he finished cooking, Annie's stomach hurt from laughing. Finally he set a plate in front of her and announced, "Be prepared to change the way you look at food."

"I think I already have," Annie said, wrinkling up her nose at her plate.

They each took a bite and then immediately spit their food across the kitchen.

Will snuck a look at Annie wiping her mouth on a napkin. He was going to miss her so much.

She pulled her cell phone out and handed it to him. "This won't work in Brazil."

Will shook his head. "No, not yet. We're only in Venezuela, Ecuador, parts of Colombia, actually mostly southern Colombia —"

"I made you something," Annie interrupted him. She pulled a handmade card out of her pocket.

Will opened it, and the card almost brought tears to his eyes. It was a drawing of the two of them with "Annie ♥ Stacks" written at the top.

"I copied your name from my phone," she explained.

Will could barely contain how much the card meant to him. He pulled her into a hug just as Grace walked in.

Grace cleared her throat. "Annie, your parents are here."

Will nodded and Guy brought the parents in.

"Annie! You ready?" her mom asked, reaching out to take Annie's bag.

Annie nodded.

"We're going right to the airport," her dad told her.

Grace bent down to look Annie in the eye. "It's been so great getting to know you. You're a special girl." She gave Annie a hug.

"You should punch Mr. Stacks in the face. So you can play in the park," Annie whispered. Grace laughed and gave Annie a kiss on the cheek.

While the others were talking, Will pulled Annie's dad aside. "I'd like to help you out," he said, pulling out his checkbook.

Annie's dad shook his head. "That's very nice of you, but we don't believe in handouts. Just hand-ups. And you already gave us one by giving us our baby back."

Will nodded. Then he turned to Annie and gave her a big hug. "Bye, Annie. Never slow your roll."

Annie nodded and then walked out with her parents and Sandy.

The door closed and everyone stood in silence for a moment. Will and Grace missed Annie already.

Eventually Guy cleared his throat and then checked his tablet. "The press is eating this up! We're going to crush. Good-bye, Harold Gray. Go back to your pathetic life as a nonprofit do-gooder."

Grace looked at Will, worried about how he was handling this. But he had already pulled out his phone. "Grace, where are we with the phone battery?" he asked.

"What?" Grace responded, surprised. How could he even think about work after everything that had happened?

"A full week on one charge. Where are we on that?" he repeated.

"We're close," she said.

"Not good enough," Will said sternly. "I'm going down to the office."

Grace put a hand on his arm. "We don't have to deal with this right now, Will," she said gently.

"Why wouldn't we?" he asked without emotion. Then he walked out the door and down to his office.

# TWENTY-TWO

Annie sat in the back of her parents' car with Sandy in a crate next to her.

"Is it cold in Brazil?" she asked as her dad pulled out into traffic and headed west.

Her mom leaned over and whispered something to her dad. He whispered back, but neither of them answered Annie. Sandy whimpered from her crate.

Meanwhile, Will was midway through a memo with Grace and Guy when there was a commotion outside of his office door. Suddenly, Nash burst in and escorted Miss Hannigan, Lou, Tessie, Isabella, Pepper, and Mia into the room.

"I'm sorry to interrupt, but I think you should hear this," Nash said.

"Annie's in trouble," Tessie blurted out.

"Those weren't her parents," Miss Hannigan said.

Grace looked from the girls to Miss Hannigan. "What's going on?" she demanded.

"Ignore her. She's clearly insane," Guy said, giving Miss Hannigan a warning look.

"Watch your mouth," Lou said threateningly.

"I made a mistake," Miss Hannigan explained. "I'm so sorry. I told him everything I knew about Annie and her parents. He found some people to pretend to be her parents. He promised me money, but I shouldn't have done it. I'm sorry."

"What do you mean those weren't her parents?" Will asked with a dreadful sinking feeling. "Where's Annie? Who offered you money?"

"He had them taken somewhere." Miss Hannigan pointed at Guy. "He's behind it all."

Will whipped around to face Guy. He couldn't believe what he was hearing.

"Where — is — Annie?" he said through clenched teeth.

In the car, Annie was getting a very bad feeling. Something was definitely off with her parents. They weren't smiling or talking to her now. They wouldn't even look at her.

She needed to get out of the car and call Will.

"Can we stop? I've got to go to the bathroom," Annie insisted.

"Just shut up," her dad snapped.

"Where are we going?" Annie asked, beginning to panic.

"We're just going to take you somewhere for a bit," her mom said. "Just relax."

"You're not my parents, are you?" Annie asked, her voice shaking.

Her mom and dad exchanged a look that Annie couldn't read. The car stopped at a red light. Annie immediately tried to open the door, but it was locked. She tried to roll down the window, but it was locked, too.

"Let me go!" Annie cried. "When Mr. Stacks finds out about this, you're —"

The man cut her off. "He doesn't need you anymore! Why do you think we're taking you?"

The woman jabbed him with her elbow. "Be quiet!"

"You work for Mr. Stacks?" Annie asked, her heart sinking. She couldn't believe it. Her eyes filled with tears and she whispered, "He wouldn't do this."

But then she thought back to the deal they had made. That she would stay with him to help his campaign. That she would take as many pictures for the press as needed.

Maybe he didn't want her around anymore. Maybe this was all just to help him win the election.

Maybe he didn't care about her after all.

Will had sprung into action. "Call my guy at the FBI. Tell him to put everyone on it," he barked to Nash. Nash headed out to make the calls.

"I'm an idiot. I didn't think anything like this would happen," Miss Hannigan whispered to Lou. She felt horrible.

"How could you not know who has her?" Will demanded of Guy.

"I have a guy who just takes care of stuff like this. It's what keeps our hands clean, trust me," Guy said, still trying to spin the situation.

"I can't trust you!" Will yelled. "You took Annie."

"I did what you told me to," Guy snapped.

"I never told you to do this," Will insisted.

Guy scoffed. "'Whatever it takes,' remember? This is just as much on you."

They all raced into the Stacks Mobile control room. The whole team had been commandeered to try to find Annie.

"Can we track her phone?" a technician asked.

"No. She gave her phone back to me." Will groaned, slamming his fist down on a console. He felt so out of control. They needed help. "Let's call the press."

"No!" Guy cried. "You're going to blow everything. Just wait until the election's over."

"What about Annie?" Pepper insisted.

"Who cares? She's just one girl," Guy exclaimed.

Hearing that made Will snap. He shoved Guy up against the wall. He was at the end of his rope. "She's all I care about!"

# TWENTY-THREE

Annie was trying not to panic, but hot tears were already rolling down her cheeks. The car pulled to a stop at another red light. Annie stared out the window. Two kids in the back of the car next to them recognized Annie. They pulled out their phones and took her picture.

"Help! Help me!" Annie yelled, banging on the window to get their attention.

"Hush!" the man snapped at her. When he realized what she was doing, he ran right through the red light to get Annie away from the kids. "Don't do anything stupid, Annie. I don't want to have to hurt you."

Annie quieted, but she had an idea. When the car

slowed again next to another car, she motioned surreptitiously out of the window until the teens in the car saw her. They instantly recognized her and whipped out their phones to take her picture.

All Annie could do was hope that someone would see the pictures and come find her.

Will and Nash stood looking at the maps for any sign of Annie, while everyone else sat and waited as patiently as possible.

"Listen to every call within the city limits," Will instructed his team of technicians.

"I *knew* you could do that," Lou gasped.

Suddenly, Isabella cried out, "Someone just posted a picture of Annie on Twitter!" She ran over to a map and pointed to a small box over one of the dots. It showed Annie crying in the back of her fake parents' car.

"Where was it taken?" Will asked.

"Fifty-Fourth and Seventh," Isabella read.

All the girls pulled out their phones and started looking for any sign of Annie on blogs, Twitter, Instagram, and Facebook.

"Another one!" Pepper yelled out. "On a gossip blog. Fifty-Sixth and Seventh!"

"They're going uptown," Will said, hurrying everyone out to his helicopter. "Let's go."

Guy, meanwhile, was still trying to salvage the campaign situation. "You do this and everyone's going to find out," he hissed. "Forget mayor. It'll destroy your whole business."

"I don't care," Will insisted.

"You're making a huge mistake! Think about everything you've worked for," Guy begged.

"That *everything* means nothing," Will said fiercely.

Guy turned to Grace. "Talk to him. You're the only one he listens to."

Grace glared at Guy . . . and then punched him in the face!

"Bam!" Pepper hollered. "That's *not* because she likes you."

Everyone except Guy hurried out to the helipad and climbed into Will's helicopter.

They took off and headed northwest.

Tessie held up her phone and announced, "Another one on Instagram. Sixty-Fifth and Tenth."

"Is anyone else dizzy?" Miss Hannigan asked,

looking green. Lou put his arm around her and patted her shoulder comfortingly.

"Just posted on the George Washington Bridge," Mia shouted.

"Go uptown!" Will ordered the pilot. Grace put her hand over his and squeezed.

"We'll find her, Will," she said.

# TWENTY-FOUR

Annie and her fake parents had turned onto the George Washington Bridge and were slowly moving in the busy traffic. She was still trying to get people to notice her, but no one in the cars around them was paying any attention — they were too distracted by the helicopter flying low over the bridge.

Annie looked up when she heard the chopper. It was Will's helicopter!

"Oh no," Annie's fake mom said, noticing it, too.

The man looked in the rearview mirror and saw a police car pulling in behind them. Its lights flashed on and the sirens wailed. There were two more police cars behind it.

Annie's fake dad yanked on the wheel and peeled off on the first exit from the bridge.

"Just let me go!" Annie wailed.

The man ignored her and sped up, racing along until he came to another police car blocking his path. He turned the wheel again and went up over the curb, crashing through some benches and driving across the lawn. The police cars followed.

Annie held on to the door and Sandy's crate tightly, her knuckles white as she tried not to be thrown across the seat as the car swerved.

"There they are!" Pepper yelled, pointing at Annie's fake parents' car below.

"Cut 'em off, bro!" Lou cheered.

Miss Hannigan whimpered. "I am crazy dizzy."

The helicopter dropped down, maneuvering right in front of the car. They were so close that Will could see Annie in the backseat. "Annie!" he yelled, desperate to get to her.

The chopper touched down, right in front of the car, forcing Annie's "dad" to slam on the brakes. He tried to reverse, but there were police cars on all sides. It was over.

The fake parents jumped out of the car and ran, but Lou tackled the man and held him down until a police officer could handcuff him. Grace grabbed the woman and shoved her right into a cop. In all the excitement, it took a moment before anyone noticed that Annie had also jumped out and was running away.

But as soon as Will saw her, he took off after her. "Annie!" He caught her midway across the bridge and pulled her to him.

Annie resisted. She blinked away her tears and turned away.

"Are you okay?" Will asked, his face filled with concern.

"I'm fine," Annie said coldly. But her lip was trembling. "We square now? You got what you needed? Want another photo?" She put her arm around him and gave a double thumbs-up and a fake smile to the reporters and photographers who had trailed the cops to the bridge. "Can I go now?"

Will shook his head. "It's not like that, honey."

"It's exactly like that," Annie said thickly. Will could hear the hurt in her voice. "We made a deal. My fault for thinking it was anything else."

"It *was* something else. It *is* something else," Will insisted.

Annie rounded on him. "You don't care about me. I was just an opportunity to you."

"That's not true!" Will exclaimed.

"It *is* true!" Hot tears streamed down Annie's face. She had been lost and betrayed so many times before. But this time hurt the most. "You did all this to me just so you could be stupid mayor."

"No," Will said. "I mean, it was that way at the beginning. But it's definitely not that way now. You've got to trust me." He refused to let her go.

"I can't trust you. I can't trust anybody!" Annie sobbed. "Just leave me alone!"

Will started crying, too. "I'm so sorry this happened to you. I can't look you in the eye and say I had nothing to do with this. But I swear to you, I did not know those weren't your real parents. You've got to believe me." He held up one finger. "This is you, Annie. This is you." He pulled her into a hug.

Annie resisted at first. But finally she gave in and hugged him back, sobbing uncontrollably.

She believed him.

When they finally pulled apart, Will kept hold of her hand. Then he turned to the growing throng of reporters. "I officially withdraw from the mayoral election," he announced. "The city needs a better person than me as its leader. I need to focus on what matters most. And that's an amazing little girl named Annie. My family."

The crowd went wild, yelling out questions and taking pictures. But Will held up his hand and shepherded Annie back over to the helicopter. He wasn't dealing with the press for a while.

"I wasn't going to vote for him anyway," Lou said, smiling.

Just outside the helicopter, Annie squeezed Will's hand. "I need one more thing from you," she said.

Will laughed. He was so grateful to have Annie back, and to have her believe in him again. "Always on the hustle, huh?" he asked. "Let's hear it."

Annie pulled up a second finger on Will's hand and then nodded to Grace. "Stop playing games."

Will smiled and let go of Annie. "That's an easy

one." Then he turned and walked over to Grace. "Not knowing what I have in front of me has been a problem of mine for a long time," he said to her. "But I'm learning." He reached out and took Grace's hand. "Will you have dinner with me?"

"What?" Grace asked, stunned.

"I can't function without you," Will said, smiling. "And I don't mean just at work. You were right about this whole mayor thing. And about Guy. And about last quarter's earnings. And about —"

Grace smiled, reached up, and kissed him. Everyone cheered.

Then Will walked Grace over to Annie and pulled them both into a hug. "Family?" he asked. Both girls nodded, and Will grinned. "Together at last."

Annie smiled wider than she ever had in her life. "Together forever!"

Reading Is
Fundamental

# READING IS SUNSHINE.
# IT MAKES YOU BRIGHT!

Reading Is Fundamental (RIF) is the largest children's literacy nonprofit on a mission to inspire children and families to love reading by providing them with free books and literacy support. **Read on. Shine on! www.RIF.org**

**In theaters December 19, 2014**

Learn more at www.annie-movie.com.